Margaret Lygnos

Poppy

Author: Lygnos, Margaret
Title: Poppy
ISBN: 978-0-646-98078-2
First published 2018
Reprinted 2022

Although this book is partly inspired by actual
events, this is a work of fiction. This story does
not seek to factually depict any actual event or
person.

A catalogue record for this
book is available from the
National Library of Australia

Editing and production by
PB Publishing, Gisborne, Victoria.

Cover photograph and photograph
on page 28 by Margaret Lygnos.

DEDICATION

My story is dedicated to three people – my uncle, the late James Aldridge, a successful author who encouraged me to keep writing, my mother-in-law Kalliopi (Poppy) who never got to Kasos, and my husband Minas who took me there.

Contents

Prologue

Poppy is the shortened name for Kalliopi.

Kalliopi was a Christian saint of the third century AD. She was executed (beheaded) in the year 250 near the beginning of Emperor Decius' violent persecution of Christians within the Roman Empire. Kalliopi was venerated in the Eastern Orthodox Church and the Roman Catholic Church. Her feast day or saint day is celebrated on June 8.

My story 'Poppy' is a work of fiction beginning with two young boys who survive a tragic event in 1824. As adults they go their separate ways. Two of their descendants meet up nearly two hundred years later and become romantically involved. The story is loosely woven around several historical events which occurred in Greece, Egypt and Australia. The characters are all fictitious.

The same names are used throughout this story to reflect Greek culture where it is customary to name the first-born son and daughter after the paternal grandparents. If Minas and Maria Pappas have a son and name him George, George's first son will be named Minas and his first daughter will be named Maria. When Minas has a son he will be named George. When George has a son he will be named Minas, etc.

This continues down the generations, keeping the family name.

Part One

Introduction

July 2010

The small Olympic aeroplane rose with ease into the clear blue sky. Poppy Mavrikakis looked down at the island of Kasos as it quickly disappeared from her view. Her eyes began to fill with tears as she thought of what she was leaving behind. She had just spent the most wonderful month of her life on the island with George, the man of her dreams, but it was over now, and she had to return to Australia.

Poppy was a vet and a partner in a practice in Greenmount, a semi-rural town near Melbourne. This had been her first overseas holiday since her parents had helped her buy into the business. Her partner Mike was managing with the help of a locum but he had been missing her experienced hands in both surgery and diagnosis. He wanted her back as soon as possible; that was the agreement and he had hinted that they should become engaged to marry when she returned.

Poppy wiped away her tears as she thought of George who had driven her to the little island airport and stayed with her until the last moment. He had held her tight and kissed her goodbye and the last thing he said to her was, "Se agapo Poppy mou" [I love you my Poppy"].

/

How it began

Crete, May 2010

Poppy Mavrikakis travelled to Crete with her friend Sophia for a well-earned holiday. They planned to spend a week with Sophia's cousins Vicky and Vasilli before deciding which other islands they would visit. Crete is a beautiful mountainous island full of rich history so the days were filled with driving and sightseeing from one end of the picturesque island to the other. One day in Elounda they were looking for a place to sit by the sea shore when two young men called out to them.

"Ella, ella, [come] Vasilli, come join us and bring the beautiful girls with you."

Poppy was a beautiful young woman with long dark hair, light olive skin and huge soft brown eyes. A pretty smile and bright personality made her even more attractive. She and her friends walked towards the two men and before anyone was introduced Poppy looked into the eyes of one of the men and felt something shift inside her. The jolt that shot through her body was not one she had ever felt before.

"Yiasou [hello]," said the man, "I am George."

"Hello, I am Poppy," she replied looking at the tall, good-looking man who grinned at her.

That was the beginning of what turned out to be one of the best days of Poppy's life. They swam in the sea and rested in the shade of a palm umbrella, chatting and laughing together. Later that night the friends walked up and down the promenade before choosing a place to eat. Even though Sophia, Vicki and Vasilli were with them, Poppy felt that she and George were in a world of their own. She was completely smitten by him and, judging by the way he looked at her, he felt the same.

They sat at a table right on the water's edge where waves lapped only metres away; the sun was setting and bouzouki music played in the background as they drank ouzo on ice and ate Greek cheese and olives.

At dinner everyone ate seafood except Poppy, who was vegetarian.

"Why don't you eat seafood?" asked George.

"Well I have always loved animals and I don't believe in eating them when it's not really necessary," she said. "Plus I am a vet and I think it's ridiculous of me to save one type of animal whilst eating another. To me they are all equal."

"Okay, I suppose that makes sense." He smiled at her. "It's easy to be a vegetarian in Greece, we have so much fresh produce available."

Poppy was not sure if he was laughing at her or not but his smile made her feel at ease. She smiled right back, looking into his eyes, and the jolt she had felt earlier that day recurred.

Several days later Poppy and George spent the day alone. They went on a boat ride from nearby Plaka which took them to an island that had once been a leper colony. The island, called Spinalonga, was both charming and poignant as remnants of the village and reminders of the people who had lived there until the 1950s were still apparent. Dilapidated little shops and dwellings opened on to narrow streets and steep stairways wound their way up the sides of buildings. The ramshackle church still had a large bell hanging over the door and the hospital, which lacked a roof, loomed over the upper part of the village. Wildflowers and weeds grew everywhere allowing colourful butterflies, bumble bees and birds to flourish. So although it was a sad place where many unfortunate people had lived their lives and died, it was full of nature's little treasures now. George proved to be a wonderful guide because of his interest in Greek history and anything to do with Hellenic culture, and he knew the island's sad story. Poppy found the whole thing fascinating as she was also from a Greek background but realised she knew very little about Greece.

Late in the afternoon they parted and went to their rooms to rest and dress for a night out together. Poppy showered and sat on the balcony to dry her hair in the sun. As she combed her hair she thought over the day and how wonderful it had been. It was barely two hours since she had left George and already she missed him.

She stopped combing her hair and stood up. "Gosh, what am I doing?" she said to herself. "I already have such strong feelings for this man. But what can come of it, he lives here and I live in Australia. What about Mike who expects to marry me? ... although I have never promised him anything."

Still talking to herself she reasoned that she was on holiday, she was not doing anything wrong and she should just enjoy the company of this wonderful man. Deep down she wondered who was kidding whom. Was it the rational Poppy or was it an impulsive Poppy she had not known existed.

Poppy put on gold sandals and a long white cotton frock which contrasted with her lightly tanned skin. She applied a little red lipstick and mascara then grabbed a shawl and went out to meet George.

His eyes lit up when he saw her. "Wow, you look very beautiful," he said.

"Thank you George, you look pretty good yourself," she smiled back at him, both excited and happy with the situation. George was tall and slim with dark wavy hair and his eyes, enhanced by thick long lashes, were a rich amber colour that glowed in contrast to his light olive complexion. He wore faded blue jeans and a white shirt which was done up almost to the top but open enough to show his bronze chest and a smattering of hair.

They sat down near the water again and shared a meal and a bottle of local wine. She told him about her work in the semi-rural town where she lived and the types of animals she treated.

"What about kangaroos?" he asked.

"Yes I do treat kangaroos and other wildlife but unfortunately it's usually when they have been injured on the road," she replied.

"What about you, George, what do you do in Crete?"

"I teach high school," said George. "History and literature mainly and I write short stories about village life on the Greek islands. I also coach a football team."

"Well we are very different aren't we," said Poppy.

"Yes but that's a good thing I think," replied George. "We can learn from each other."

As the night progressed and they asked and answered questions of each other, Poppy felt herself drawing closer and closer to George; there was a spark between them that threatened to burst into a flame. George moved nearer and pulling her towards him they shared their first kiss. Poppy melted at the touch of his soft lips on hers and coupled with the sensation of his firm chest pressing against her breasts she wanted the embrace to go on and on. He felt warm and his recently showered body smelled wonderfully of the sun, the sea and of masculinity.

"I have wanted to kiss you from the first moment I saw you," said George.

"Me too," Poppy said softly, moving towards him and kissing him again.

"Can I come up to your room tonight Poppy?" Poppy was almost out of breath due to the kiss and what he was asking but she answered, "I am tempted, but no, I don't want to get too involved with you; it would be too difficult for me to walk away."

They finished their dinner and George suggested a walk along the sand to an outcrop of rocks where they sat with their feet in the water and looked at the moon rising. After many passionate kisses Poppy toyed with the idea of inviting George to her room after all but as they returned to the road and began to walk back to the hotel, George told her that unfortunately, tomorrow he had to fly to his home on the island of Kasos where his family had a taverna.

"I always go and help out during the summer," he said. "And I am always happy to do it, but now that I have met you I don't want to go."

Poppy stopped and looked up at him. "See? That's exactly why I don't want to get too involved with you. If we become lovers tonight I will get hurt." She felt angry, hurt and sad all at once.

He pulled her to him and kissed her again then he whispered in her ear, "Poppy would you come to Kasos when you leave Crete?"

"Oh – I wasn't expecting that," she replied.

"Well, why not come to Kasos? It's a beautiful quiet island, not too many tourists and it has a very interesting history. We could spend hours and hours together getting to know each other. Please come."

Poppy thought about what he was suggesting for just one heartbeat then said, "yes, I will come to Kasos."

2

Poppy goes to Kasos

Getting off the ferry in Kasos, Poppy looked around the small port and to the nearby white buildings. Behind the little square dwellings there were huge brown mountains which seemed to surround the quaint village of Free. The aqua sea was smooth and sparkling and a small flock of seagulls swooped at something floating on the surface. Little fishing boats were lined up at the port and two large yachts were settled just offshore in the calm water. There was an open-fronted cafe up on a hill to the right of the port and she could see people sitting drinking coffee and children eating ice-creams nearby.

Poppy had a hand-sketched map that George had given her pointing out rooms to let and the road to his family's taverna. She crossed the road and booked into a room that had a wonderful view of the sea and across to another island on the horizon. She stood on the balcony watching several fishermen on the port cleaning fish and throwing scraps to the gulls. Others were mending their nets and talking loudly to each other. They sounded as though they were arguing but Poppy knew they were simply talking loudly in the excited animated way most Greek men did.

It was late morning when she set off down the road towards the taverna where she hoped to find George. As she walked she realised she did not even know his surname, or the name of the taverna. On the map he had drawn three buildings with a cross beneath, not clearly indicating one or the other. Poppy half expected George to be waiting for her but she also thought 'what if he was not, what if he had not really wanted or cared if she came to his island of Kasos'. But she was on the island and she definitely wanted to see him so she strode with purpose down the road.

The wide road followed the seashore on one side and was lined with stone fences on the other. She heard bleating and looked over a fence to where a small herd of goats tried to shelter from the hot sun. The unfortunate goats stumbled on the hard rocky earth because their front and back legs were tied together to prevent them from running, jumping or climbing. There was hardly any shade, very little water and no visible food.

"Oh you poor things," said Poppy. "This is so cruel. Next time I come down here I will bring scissors and cut that rope. You should be running free."

Further along the road she saw a turkey with two little chicks scratching in the weeds; when they heard her approach they quickly ran under their mother's legs for protection. The mother turkey promptly sat on the chicks, spreading her wings over them, and stared at Poppy with a look that said 'don't you dare'.

"I won't hurt you," Poppy said, slowly moving away from the frightened birds. Fancy seeing turkeys roaming free; that's a first, she said to herself.

Up ahead between the road and the shore there was a very old windmill which had lost its blades. It appeared that someone had been doing some restoration work on the little building as there was paint and timber at the door and a ladder leaning against the wall.

"Oh I love the look of that!" Poppy said to herself. She walked over to the stone building and pushed open the weatherbeaten door, which was slightly ajar. Inside it was dark but as her eyes became accustomed to the dark she could see the work that had been carried out. The walls had been resurfaced and whitewashed, the window and door frames appeared to be new and a small area had been partitioned off and turned into a small shower room. Wooden frames suggested a mezzanine floor was to be added over one half of the floor space.

"This is so quaint," said Poppy to herself. "All it needs is a little kitchen and I could live in here, it is so charming and right on the seashore."

She closed the door behind her and continued along the road. Rounding the corner she arrived at a pretty beach within a small bay. Facing the sea was a house and two tavernas, both very alike and each one with Greek writing above the entrance. There were two people sunning themselves on the beach and four children playing and calling out to each other in the shallow water. Poppy turned her gaze to the buildings facing the sea and noticed that in the first taverna there was a woman setting tables, otherwise there was no-one else around.

"How on earth can I tell which one is his?" thought Poppy. "Damn this, it's really silly of me to come all this way and I don't really know where I am going or what I am doing. I'll just have to ask."

She walked up to the first taverna and spoke to the woman setting the tables.

"Kali spera." (Good afternoon) said the woman.

"Kali spera. I am looking for George," said Poppy.

"Which George?" The woman laughed. "There are many men called George on Kasos."

"Well this one is young and he is a teacher," said Poppy.

"Ah, that's next door," She replied. "Good luck."

Poppy walked next door. She couldn't see George but she went in and sat down. Two pretty little cats with small triangular faces came to her table and looked up at her hopefully. Poppy patted one and scratched the head of the other. The cats responded in an affectionate manner knowing they had met a cat lover.

An attractive middle-aged woman smiled at Poppy as she put a glass of water on the table and handed her a menu.

Poppy looked at the menu and ordered a tiropita (cheese pie).

When the food was brought to the table Poppy looked up at the woman and said, "Thank you. I am looking for George, is he here?"

"Do you mean my son?" said the woman.

"Maybe, I am not sure, I met him recently in Crete."

"Yes, George was in Crete last week, but he is out with a friend now, his girlfriend."

"He has a girlfriend?"

"Yes, they have been together for a long time."

Poppy felt herself blush. How could she have been so silly, so naive. She had left her friend Sophia in Crete with her cousins which she knew was not right and now she would have to go back with her tail between her legs.

Her appetite was gone. She left money on the table and walked out fuming, back up the road to Free.

3

Poppy and George in Kasos

Back in her room she looked on the internet to see how soon she could get off the island and away from the biggest mistake of her life. She discovered there was a plane that came daily on which she could book a seat and escape within the next few days. She felt humiliated and really angry with herself, now seeing the impulsive Poppy had made a bad decision. The day was hot, a swim would have been nice but she didn't want to risk seeing George so she settled for another shower and lay on her bed and tried to read. She found it difficult to concentrate on the book and gave up, finding sleep was almost impossible.

Poppy had gone to bed without eating either lunch or dinner so on rising the next morning she was very hungry and had to go out for breakfast. At the nearby cafe she drank her coffee and picked up her phone preparing to ring Sophia to tell her what had happened and to expect to see her soon. A hand touched her shoulder and she looked up to see George grinning at her.

"Kali mera, Poppy mou (good morning my Poppy)," you came, I am so happy to see you," he said as he sat at her table.

"I am not your Poppy," she said angrily. "Your mother told me you have a girlfriend; I left my friend in Crete to come here to be with you and you are already involved with someone else. I am so angry and I am leaving as soon as I can get on the plane."

George took Poppy's hand. "No Poppy, it's not true, I don't have a girlfriend. She is just a friend who my mother would like me to marry but I am not interested in her, especially now that I have met you."

Poppy wanted to believe him and he certainly looked as though he was telling the truth, but was he?

"I think we had better have a good talk," said Poppy.

"Look she is not my girlfriend. I have known her since we were children and our parents are very close but there has never been anything but friendship between us.

"Do you swear it?"

"Yes I do."

"Yes but what your mother said --"

He cut her off. "My mother wants something that I will not agree to. That's the end of it," he said convincingly.

Poppy looked at George; she heard what he said and she wanted to believe him. She decided she had come so far she would give him the benefit of the doubt.

"Okay I will stay for a week and during that time you will have to convince me," she said finally.

"I have to work until three; come to our taverna for lunch and then we can talk," said George. "Then I will drive you around my beautiful island and I will do my best to persuade you of my intentions."

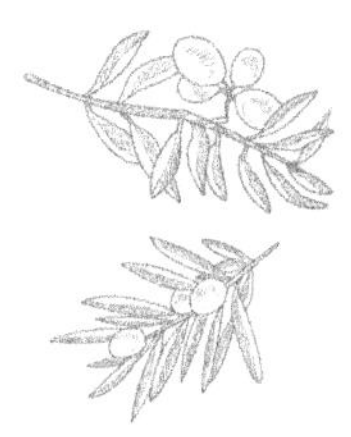

4

Getting to know each other

"George I don't even know your surname," Poppy said.

"It's Mavrikakis," replied George.

"Really?" said Poppy. "That's my name also."

"Well it is a common name in Greece and particularly here on Kasos."

"Yes but don't you think that's a big deal?"

"We could be distantly related," laughed George.

"I hope it's a very great distance!" said Poppy.

"There are Mavrikakis' everywhere," he said. "Many people left Kasos in the late nineteenth century and went to live and work in Egypt. Eventually they left Egypt and went all over the world – to America, Canada, Australia and some to Athens."

"So this is probably where my family name originates," said Poppy. "My Mavrikakis must have gone to Australia. When I ring my father I will ask him what he knows about Kasos."

George brought a Greek salad, spanakopita and tzajiki to the table.

"This looks delicious, did you cook it?" Poppy asked.

"I helped my mother," he replied. "She and my father both cook for the taverna."

Poppy tasted the spanakopita. "This tastes the same as those my yiayia used to make. The pastry is thick and my mother always said yiayia couldn't make pastry but it's just a different type of pastry. I like it."

"This is Kasos pastry, that's the way we like it."

As they sat and talked, George's mother brought fish scraps out to feed the stray cats.

"Mupss, mupss," she called to them.

"My papou (grandfather) says mupss, mupss to call the cats and I have never heard it anywhere else," said Poppy. "Another coincidence and another thing to tell my father."

5

Getting to know the island

The afternoon was beginning to cool as Poppy and George drove off and headed for the village of Poli which was halfway up and in between two mountains. They parked the car near a very old church. "There is a festival here next week, we will go if you like," said George.

"What type of festival?"

"It's a religious festival, a saint's day, we have a lot here on Kasos, it's always lots of fun. We eat and drink and dance," he replied. "Oh and there is a church service first."

Poppy approached the church fence and peered through the gate. The courtyard was paved with black and white polished stones which had been placed flat sides together in decorative formations leading up to the church and through the doors to the inside of the building. Several cats slept on the stone steps in the sunshine and a ginger kitten was chewing a piece of octopus. In the distance the sound of bleating goats could be heard.

Poppy turned to look at the surrounding view and was astounded at the sight of the drystone walls that were everywhere. They stretched horizontally in tiers all over the side of the vast mountains; mountains whose immense size dwarfed the little village. Far and wide she could see walls that had been built by hand, stone after stone, hundreds of years ago. She was amazed at the beauty of these walls and conscious of the hard work that must have gone into creating them.

"These areas were all farmed once," said George. "The walls were built to terrace the mountainside and create flat land for farming and to distinguish ownership of the land. They were so well built they are still standing today."

"They are fascinating. They really add to the beauty and mystery of the mountains," said Poppy.

They drove for more than an hour up steep single-lane roads, through herds of goats grazing on the roadside; stopping to look down at the tiny village by the sea, occasionally taking a break to snap photos of the scenery or pat a baby donkey. Birds of prey, which Poppy thought to be falcons, soared high into the blue sky seeking their next meal.

"Now I will take you to my village," said George.

They drove to Agia Marina, a bigger village with pretty houses, meandering narrow streets and a big church. As they walked along the streets Poppy saw some of the houses were so close together that the women could sit in their own living rooms and chat to each other across the walkway. George said "Yiasou" to several people as they passed their windows. White hand-crocheted curtains hung at most of the open windows.

The church bells began to ring and further up the road they saw a small procession approaching the church. Several women all dressed in black supported a middle-aged woman who was crying noisily and appeared to be on the point of collapse. Following them on the back of an old red farm truck was a glossy timber coffin held securely by half a dozen sad-looking men.

"I know this woman," said George, as he crossed himself. "Her mother died just two days ago."

"How sad," said Poppy. "It looks so different from how it is done in my country."

Walking away from the church George said, "This is our family home." He pointed to a white two-storey house with dark blue trimmings. Red geraniums grew in window boxes and a magnificent purple bougainvillea climbed up to the roof. There was a white stone fence with blue gate surrounding a small shaded garden.

"Oh, how charming," said Poppy.

"Yes it is, my mother is very proud of her house and garden."

"I can see more and more why you are so fond of Kasos, it's very appealing."

"I love Kasos and I hope you'll grow to love it too," said George. They drove in silence for a while just enjoying the quiet. "Your island is rugged and rustic and so beautiful," said Poppy. "I think I could get to love your island."

That night after dinner Poppy took George back to her hotel room. They sat together on the balcony enjoying the view until the sun went down.

"Let's go in now Poppy because I want to make love to you," said George. "I want you very much."

Poppy looked at him and smiled as she stretched her hand out to his. Without a word she stood up and led him inside. They stood beside the bed and kissed slowly, then drew back to look into each other's eyes and began to undress. Although they had seen each other at the beach in their bathing costumes this was now so different, so erotic, and suddenly the mood changed and they were pulling their remaining clothes off and falling onto the bed desperate to be joined in that wonderful way that new lovers are. Poppy opened her eyes and looked up at George who gazed down at her as he moved inside her. With their eyes locked together they reached the high point of their lovemaking together.

6

Falling in love with George and Kasos

Poppy stayed after the first week without broaching the subject, it was just an unspoken agreement. The couple spent all of George's spare time together and when he was working Poppy passed her time at the beach. Sitting in the shallows she would feed bread crumbs to the tiny fish that swam just below the surface of the water. Then she would swim out further and float on her back gazing up at the beautiful mountains which intrigued her more each day. It was not just their colour and size but the number of terraced drystone walls which were everywhere she looked. She began to wonder about the people who had toiled to build them. Sometimes she imagined she could see the islanders of long ago leading their donkeys up the mountainside or attending the vegetables growing in the hot sun. One of these visions seemed to be a small family coming slowly down the mountain leading a donkey. They appeared to stop and then next she could see them returning up the mountain track. How different their lives must have been, thought Poppy; simple, hard lives farming to feed hungry mouths. They would have been so dependent on a good rainfall and continued good health, their lives in the lap of the gods. Another day she thought she saw the same family coming down the mountainside, a man leading a donkey followed by a woman with a baby strapped to her upper body and trailed by two small children. They seemed to stop at the same place as before, then the last she saw of them was the backside of the donkey as they walked back up the mountain.

She knew there were goats up there but she could not see them from the beach – the lucky goats that were able to graze freely as they had in the past, more fortunate than the hobbled goats that Poppy had tried to talk to George about. He had just shrugged his shoulders and said some of them would run away if they were not hobbled.

Then there were the cats that were everywhere, not really belonging to anyone, sleeping in the sun or growling at each other at night. She loved the look of the cats, which were small with pretty triangular faces and huge appealing eyes, the tiny kittens mewing and following their mothers into rubbish bins looking for something to eat.

"They look like the cats on Egyptian drawings," Poppy remarked to George one day.

"They look the same because that's where they are from originally. They have been here for as long as anyone can remember."

"How do they survive?"

"Some people love them and feed them every day. One man on the island carries cat food in his car and when the cats see the car driving along they recognise it and run after it until he stops. He feeds them every day."

"I think if I lived here I would become known as the cat woman," Poppy replied. "I would also feed them and I would like to do something to stop them breeding."

"Well, we are doing something...we raise money to pay for veterinary students to come to Kasos once or twice a year to neuter them, so there are fewer cats than there once were."

Poppy was quite good at drawing and favoured animals as subjects so in her spare time she began sketching the Kasos cats. They were quite easy to draw because of their angular faces and straight sleek bodies. When George saw her pictures he was full of admiration.

"You are quite an artist," he said.

"It runs in the family, my father is an art teacher and his father and grandfather were both artists. We have a lot of their paintings and drawings hanging in our homes."

She also drew a picture of the family walking down the mountain with the donkey which George found very odd.

"No one uses donkeys on the island now," said George.

"I think you are wrong," said Poppy. "I have seen the same family with a donkey on the mountainside more than once."

"Where was that?"

"I can show you exactly." Poppy pointed to the area on the mountain where she had seen the little family. "They came around that corner between those two big rocks."

"I thought so," said George. "Those people are not really there – some of us can see them but most cannot."

"What do you mean? Are they imaginary people?" asked Poppy.

"I don't know, I just know that sometimes some people see a family with a donkey and several children coming down the mountain but they never get down here. Many times after a sighting people have rushed up the track to see them but there is never anyone to see."

"How strange, I wonder why I have seen them."

"It's usually only people who are visiting Kasos who see them, not often the islanders. There are all sorts of theories about who they are, the most popular idea is that they are a family trying to return to their village but are forced back up the mountain by something unpleasant ahead of them."

"What do you mean, something unpleasant?"

"A terrible thing happened here in 1824, many of the Kasiots were killed by invaders who arrived in a fleet of ships and it changed everything about the island completely – maybe they are from that time."

George told Poppy a little about the event and took her to the edge of a rocky hillside to point out the date **'1824'** written in stones just above the shoreline which could be viewed properly from the sea.

"This is to remind us of what happened on our island and in memory of all the people who lost their lives," he said.

7

Good intentions backfire

Poppy had been feeding two small cats that hung around the rooms she was renting. A male and a female, probably brother and sister because they were very alike. Poppy was about to feed them one day when she observed that the little female appeared to be pregnant. She picked her up and palpated the abdomen, where she felt two kittens moving inside.

"Oh dear, two more little ones will be here soon, you poor wee things."
She placed the food down and the cats devoured it quickly.

Later that day Poppy decided it was time to cut the ropes on the hobbled goats' legs. She had been to see them most days, feeding and talking to them and hoping to get their confidence, but they were still scared of her. Tonight is the night, she decided one evening when George was working, so she walked determinedly down the path, scissors in hand, to where the goats were kept within a very unappealing enclosure. The path was much higher than the area in which the goats were kept so it was a bit tricky to get down to them. First she had to climb over a weird fence made of stones, old pieces of wood, tin cans and barbed wire. Finding it very difficult to get over the obstacles without hurting herself on the barbed wire she lost her grip on the stones and fell head first into the yard causing the goats to scatter in all directions. She scrabbled to her feet and crept slowly after the goats but they continued to avoid her. Sitting on the ground in the dirt she scattered some food and eventually, after a lot of coaxing and patience, a few goats came close enough for her to grab. She managed to cut the ropes on only two of the goats as the others just kept running away from her in fright. The animals made quite a bit of noise and just when she decided it was time to give up, someone came to the fence, probably alerted by the noise. Fortunately it was nearly dark so Poppy, who pressed herself right up against the fence in the dirt and goat droppings, was not seen and the person went away. Defeated, she scrambled back over the fence, falling again and grazing both knees on the rough stones of the path. As she scrubbed herself under the shower she wondered if she would tell George and whether he might be angry with her.

Later that night she did tell George about her attempts to free the goats and how she had almost been caught. He was not cross, he was very amused and laughed out loud every time he thought about her falling over the fence into goat poo, scaring and scattering the goats she was trying to liberate.

"That's the funniest thing I have heard for a long time, I wish I had seen you." He had another big laugh which made Poppy laugh too.

******

Goat Gossip

Today my goat sisters and I were just sitting and dozing in the sun like we do every day when a two-leg fell into our pen. It had food but it also had a sharp, shiny thing and it chased us trying to get between our back legs. It was after our milk so we kept running away. It didn't get our milk but it did cut the restricters on two of my sisters. We were all glad when the silly two-leg fell out of our pen and it left the food behind. We ate the food and went back to sleep in the sun.

******

8

Festivities

On Saturday night George took Poppy to the festival of the Holy Trinity at Poli. Poppy went into the church to watch the service where five priests dressed in magnificent robes sang and chanted to a handful of keen worshippers. Most of the villagers crept into the church, quickly crossed themselves, lit a candle and hurried outside to sit in the cool night air and chat with their friends. One of the priests blessed several large rustic loaves of bread which were finally taken outside to be cut up and shared with everyone. A wonderful free meal of dolmathes, rice and meat was provided to everyone present and homemade wine, also free, was offered. There was an enormous number of small flies buzzing around the food and annoying everyone.

"I thought we had a fly problem in Australia!" said Poppy.

"Don't worry," said George, "the flies will go to bed soon."

After everyone had eaten, local musicians began to play the island music and several men sang folk songs from Kasos. Eventually there was a call from the musicians for the women to get up and dance.

"Elate yinekes elate, na horepsete [come women, come, dance]." The women began to dance in the typical Greek style, holding hands and circling the floor. The steps were graceful, delicate and feminine and they all danced with ease, heads held high, smiling at each other. Poppy could not sit still, she had to get to her feet and join the line of women and girls to dance with them. Although she had never danced these particular steps before she persevered, keeping her eye on the leader until she mastered the dance and eventually was in step with the other women.

"I am surprised that you can dance Greek style," said George.

"It's because my father is Greek and I have socialised with Greek people all my life," Poppy replied.

The men joined in the dancing and George led a line of dancers around the courtyard of the church.

When they sat down George took Poppy to where his parents were sitting. Poppy had not met George's father yet as he was always in the kitchen cooking.

"Poppy, this is my father, Minas Mavrikakis," said George.

"Hello," said Poppy. "Did George tell you that my family surname is Mavrikakis and my papou is Minas?"

"Yes; our name is very old and is common on the island of Kasos," said Minas as he smiled and held out his hand to Poppy. "It is the tradition for us to name the first son after the paternal grandfather. Sometimes it can get a bit confusing because there can be many people in the same family with the same name."

"Yes I know," said Poppy. "But your name and surname is the same as in my family, a very big coincidence to my way of thinking."

"Well it's possible your family has the same roots as ours," said Minas.

"I keep saying I will ring my father to ask him about all these coincidences," said Poppy, "now I really must speak to him." George's mother, although not directly rude to Poppy, said very little to her, preferring to speak in Greek to the people sitting near her.

The night was warm and a slight breeze wafted over the gathering. A huge full moon rose over the mountain and the flies which had been present in swarms suddenly disappeared. The festival continued late into the night but Poppy and George, wanting to be alone, left at midnight. As they left George's mother said something that Poppy did not understand.

George replied to his mother. "Stamata ma ola ine endaxie [Stop Mum it's all okay]."

"What is wrong?" said Poppy.

"Just the same old thing," he replied.

9

Last days

Poppy did ring her father at last to ask if they had a connection to Kasos and, no surprise to her, he said yes. "It is a very sad story and my grand-parents never wanted to talk about it," he said. "I suppose I just followed their lead."

Over the last two weeks of Poppy's stay on Kasos the couple fell more in love and both knew they wanted to be together, but where and how they could not agree.

"I can't stay here because although there is work for a vet it's not much and will not pay well, plus I have a business partner waiting for my return," said Poppy. "And I owe my parents a lot of money which they lent to me to buy into the practice."

"Well I can't leave my teaching job on Crete either," said George.

"You could teach in Australia," urged Poppy. "A friend of my father teaches in a Greek school in Melbourne and they are always looking for good teachers."

"You have Greek schools in Melbourne?" asked George.

"Of course, Melbourne is the third-largest Greek-speaking city in the world after Athens and Thessaloniki," replied Poppy.

"Really, I didn't know that," said George. "Are you sure?"

"Yes, you can check on the internet if you doubt me."

They could not resolve the problem of who would move – it just seemed too hard. However they did decide that George would fly to Australia in his next term break to see Poppy and perhaps, having been apart for so long, it would force them to come to some decision that would solve the dilemma.

The little cat had her kittens, two tiny white fluffy scraps with black and brown patches. She was a devoted mother who hid the kittens but Poppy searched until she found them and fed them in the hiding place.

As they were having dinner together on Poppy's last night, George said he had a surprise for Poppy.

"I have something very special to show you after dinner."

"A surprise! I love surprises."

It was dark when they left the tavern and began to stroll up the road to Free. They had not gone far when George put his arm around Poppy and steered her off the road towards the old windmill by the sea.

"This is my surprise for you," he said as he opened the door.

Poppy gasped, "Oh George, is this your place?"

"Yes. My father and I have been working on it for ages and now it's finished and ready for occupation and you and I are going to occupy it tonight."

Poppy peered into the dimly lit interior. On the mezzanine floor George had placed a bed which faced a window looking out to sea. In the downstairs area there was a little table, two chairs and a cupboard which opened to reveal a small kitchenette. A few paintings on the wall and a vase of wildflowers on the windowsill made the place comfortable and inviting. An array of small candles in various places shed a soft romantic light over the room.

They climbed up to the bed and George said, "We can leave the window open and listen to the sea all night and then watch the sun rise in the morning."

"Oh George, this is perfect." Poppy was close to tears. "You are making it so much harder for me to leave."

The last night together was bittersweet. Their slow and passionate lovemaking had already become a beautiful harmonised experience which neither of them had ever known before. Night turned to day as they slipped into an exhausted sleep.

Poppy woke first and stood naked at the window watching the waves break on the seashore and George lay on the bed looking at the silhouette of the beautiful girl who had stolen his heart and was leaving him today.

10

Back home

Poppy met up with her friend Sophia at Athens airport and they travelled home together. Sophia was really pleased that Poppy was in love with George and hoped that he felt the same; she didn't consider it just a holiday romance but she kept that to herself.

On her return home Poppy was extremely busy, having to take up four days a week of consulting and two days on call every second weekend. This did not allow her time to mope and feel sorry for herself but George was always at the back of her mind and there when she had time to sit and think or just before she fell asleep each night.

Mike seemed a bit on edge when Poppy first returned to the practice; he embraced her and said he was glad she was back at last but no more. At the end of her first week back she could see that something was bothering Mike and knew she had to tell him about George as soon as possible but kept waiting for the right moment. As it turned out she didn't have to wait too long.

The locum, Andrea, who had filled in for Poppy, seemed to hang around a lot but as she had a week before her next job began, Poppy thought little of it. One afternoon Poppy arrived early to take over from Mike and walked into the office to find Mike and Andrea in a very intimate embrace. Backing out to give them their privacy she did not know if she should laugh or cry. Quickly Mike came out blushing and began to apologise.

"I'm sorry Poppy, it just happened, I feel awful and I didn't want you to find out this way. Andrea is a wonderful person and I just fell for her."

"It's okay Mike, this makes it easier for me to tell you something that has been on my mind ever since I came home."

Poppy told Mike about George. They talked openly and both of them realised they were happy for the other. They embraced and called Andrea out of the office. Andrea looked nervously at Poppy as she emerged but Poppy reassured her that it was all okay and asked Mike to tell her about George.

When Poppy told her parents about George and the coincidence of the names her father said he would talk to his parents to see what they knew about Kasos. They were happy that Poppy was in love but were concerned at the prospect of her going to live in Greece.

Poppy engrossed herself in her work and spoke to George every few days. He said he was missing her and had booked his flight to Australia. She was thrilled to hear that news but still felt she wouldn't believe it until she saw him at Tullamarine airport in Melbourne.

Meanwhile George returned to his teaching job on Crete without telling his parents of his intention to travel to Australia. He didn't want an argument so he kept putting it off.

When his mother asked him if he would be coming home on his next term break he was given the perfect opportunity.

"No," he said, "I am going to Australia to see Poppy."

"Don't be ridiculous," his mother said. "Nothing can come of that relationship."

"We want to be together and we have to work out how we can be," he replied.

"Oh George, no, I can't bear it, I won't allow it," said his poor mother. "You know we have always hoped you would marry Athina Pappas."

"Yes I know but I don't want to marry Athina," he answered.

"George, go to Australia if you must, have an affair with that girl and then come back to marry Athina."

"Mum, stamata, [quiet] I have made up my mind to be with Poppy either here or in Australia and that's the end of it." For the first time in his life George hung up the phone while his mother was still talking.

Memorial
on Kasos.

11

How it really began

Kasos, June 7, 1824

On 7th June 1824, Minas and Maria Mavrikakis arose early; the sun was just edging over the top of the mountain as they began the climb to reach their little plot of land. When Minas was not fishing he went weekly up the mountain to tend his vegetable garden and check on his goat herd. Sometimes he took Maria and the children with him and they would take a picnic lunch and spend a family day together. Today Maria's brother Stavros who lived nearby, his wife Soula and their little girl Eleni were going with them.

Maria led their donkey with little Christos riding high on its back. Although he was a robust little boy of about eighteen months his little legs would hinder their ascent. Their other son, George, ran ahead to Maria's brother's house to let him know they were on their way.

Stavros and Soula were waiting on their doorstep with little Eleni who jumped up and down with excitement. Soula, who was expecting a baby soon, sat on their donkey ready to ride up the steepest part of the climb.

It was a beautiful warm morning. Plump thyme bushes covered in purple flowers grew everywhere, saturating the air with a wonderful scent. The colour of the herb gave the hills a soft mauve hue which contrasted beautifully with the rocky brown soil. The aroma of the thyme filled their lungs as they breathed deeply with the exertion of climbing.

The two men talked together as they led the way up the slopes followed by George and Eleni. The two children laughed and skipped from place to place looking for adventure.

"Ella, ella [come, come]," called little George who was poking a stick into a rabbit hole.

"No, leave them George," said his mother. "We do not need rabbits today but we might another day, you never know what God has in store for us."

Maria was a sensible woman who had learned from a very young age to appreciate all that they had and not to waste anything, so she would not allow an animal to be killed unless they needed it. She was very fond of her sister-in-law Soula and was looking forward to another niece or nephew but mostly she hoped for a healthy mother and baby and a quick, uncomplicated delivery.

Maria held the reins and led both the donkeys so she and Soula could talk about the plans for the baby.

"I hope so much for a boy this time," said Soula. "And many more babies in the future."

"Let's get this one here safely first," said Maria.

The little group followed the track for another half hour, the men engrossed in a political discussion about the desire for freedom of Greece from Turkish rule; the children chatting together and the women still talking about babies, when suddenly Soula cried out.

"Something is happening, I have some pain — can you call Stavros. I think it's the baby."

Maria called out to Stavros: "Soula is feeling unwell and is having some pain; we will have to stop here for a while."

Stavros lifted Soula from the donkey and put her on the ground out of the hot sun to rest.

Soula begged Stavros to take her home. Her first baby had been born very quickly and she wanted to be in her own bed with the midwife by her side as soon as possible.

"We will stay here for a while and when you have rested I will take you home," said Stavros. "Eleni can still go with Minas and Maria. She was really looking forward to spending the day with George and Christos."

Maria offered to stay with Soula but Stavros thought it better that he stayed so that he could take her home if she was in labour.

"Okay," said Maria. "We will call in to see you on the way home and bring Eleni this evening."

Maria did not like leaving Soula but she had the three children to keep an eye on now so she continued with Minas up the steep track.

Little Christos was now off the donkey and scrambling up the track, falling often but quickly getting to his feet to try to keep up with the other two. The family stopped now and then to talk to other people who were going up or down the mountain. Some of their neighbours who were not accompanied by their children overtook them and teased them about how long it would take them to get to their destination. Maria did not mind because her children were her life and she enjoyed every moment she spent with them.A cool breeze blew up from the sea as they reached the top of the mountain and crossed a small plateau to descend into a valley. The area was green and lush with olive trees planted in rows on the side of the hill and fig trees providing enormous areas of shade. Wildflowers which grew everywhere buzzed with insects and tiny birds.

The sound of goat bells could be heard in the distance and when Minas began to call out, goats appeared from all directions. He took fresh grass from bags on the donkey's back and spread it around. This way when the goats came to eat he was able to identify his and count how many new kids (baby goats) had been born. He put his identifying bells on his new kids and chose a young nanny goat with a full udder and two healthy male kids at her side. Minas tied a rope around the nanny goat and tied her to the donkey and the two kids stayed by her side.

"One of the kids we will eat and the other we can sell," he said. "And the katchika [nanny] can join our milking herd at home to provide us with more milk for our cheese making."

The children played with the kids which were very playful and loved running and skipping in the grass but would not go far from their mother.

The family sat in the shade of a fig tree and Maria brought out bread and cheese for the family to eat for lunch. After the meal the two older children lay down to sleep while Minas went to check on his vegetables and bee hives.

Maria stayed under the tree with little Christos who settled on her lap and began to feed from his mother's breast. Maria loved these moments alone with her little son who lay in her arms and looked up at her with absolute adoration. His plump little hand patted her breast and she stroked his cheek and sang softly to him as he dropped off to sleep. The older two children were fast asleep now and one of them quietly snored. Nearby the donkey slept, its nose almost touching the ground, and the two young goats nudged at their mother's udder taking it in turns to feed.

Minas went to his family plot which, like all the others, was enclosed by drystone walls. Bee hives were along one side and the remainder of the rich red soil was planted with vegetables. Minas pulled out weeds, hoed the soil and picked vegetables which he placed in baskets that the donkey would carry home for them. The bees buzzed around the hive. Minas looked up and watched a falcon soaring above him; it stopped and hovered before swooping to the ground to pick up a mouse in its strong talons.

He looked at the rustic scene and felt content with his life and all it entailed. What a wonderful place this is and I am such a fortunate man to live here with my family, he thought to himself. Everything is as it should be, and he turned to rejoin his family.

He walked back to where the family lay under the tree and gazed with love and pride at his two strong sons, his niece and his beautiful wife.

"We will start back when the children wake," he said to Maria.

12

On the mountain

The descent was easy once they climbed out of the valley and crossed the plateau towards the downward track. From the top of the mountain there was a view of the sea far below. The sea sparkled as usual and there was a fine heat haze covering the village near the port. Minas glanced down and then he took a second look.

"Look Maria, there are strange ships in the port."

Maria looked where he pointed. "Who are they and why so many?"

"I don't know, we were not expecting ships and there really are too many to count. It does not look right – this is very odd."

They remained where they were for some time discussing who the strangers might be and wondering what to do: should they stay put or should they continue towards home?

Minas decided to go a little further down to see if he could see better. He returned looking very worried.

"I did not go very far so it was difficult to see but there is indeed a large fleet of ships and I am not sure who they belong to. I think we should not go home until we know who they are and what is happening." He turned to the children.

"Come children, we are not going home yet; we will stay up on the mountain tonight."

The children were thrilled at the prospect of a night out in the open and turned and raced back along the track where they had come from.

George and Eleni almost collided with a young family like their own who approached them intending to return down the track to their village. Minas stopped to speak to them.

"Something strange is happening down there," he said to the couple. "We are going to stay up here tonight."

He drew the man aside to where they could view the port together and after a brief discussion he agreed with what Minas was saying and decided he and his family would remain up on the mountain also. Following that they met several other families who also decided to stay put. It was summer time so the nights were warm and there was little chance of rain. Even so, Minas decided to keep his family sheltered and hidden. There were many caves in the mountains so the family settled inside one for the night.

"Tomorrow we will see what is happening," said Minas as he settled down and tried to sleep. He was worried for his family and all sorts of thoughts went through his head. Minas and Maria put the children between them to make them feel more secure. Maria slept a little but Minas not at all. Never before had he seen so many ships come to Kasos and this left him feeling uneasy and suspicious. The things that ran through his mind were too awful to contemplate.

The next day Maria made a simple meal from the leftover cheese and bread and tried to make their second day on the mountain an adventure for the children, who ran and rolled about the little valley picking wildflowers and chasing huge red and yellow butterflies. While the children played Minas and one of the other men ventured down just a little to see what was happening in the village. They were still very high up and were careful not to be seen and when they returned Minas said very little to Maria, only that they did not appear to be friendly people, whoever they were.

"We will remain here for the time being," he said.

Minas had recognised most of the ships as Egyptian because a few had been in the port for a short time recently. The others he thought were Turkish and he worried about what was taking place on his beloved island of Kasos.

13

Sadness

Maria wanted to cook over a fire but Minas would not allow it in case the smoke was detected so they had to settle for raw vegetables and goat's milk – fortunately there was plenty of both. It was almost impossible to collect water as there was no rain, just a fine mist at night, so although they left a bowl out at night they collected only a few drops. Fortunately they were used to drinking goat's milk.

During the second week Minas decided that when it was dark he would walk halfway down the mountain hoping to get some idea of what was happening. The children were sleeping when Minas returned well after midnight. When Maria looked at him in the moonlight she could see he was carrying something small inside his shirt. As he drew nearer she could see that his face looked haggard and tear-stained. He sat next to her and she felt him shudder.

Whatever it was he carried inside his shirt moved and made a weak mewing sound. Minas could not speak, as he brought out from his shirt a tiny, skinny, newborn baby.

"The-e-mou! [my god]," said Maria. "What have you here?"

Minas put the baby into Maria's arms.

"Feed the baby Maria, she is weak and starving, I promised Soula we would care for her."

Maria took the baby and put it under her blouse next to her warm skin. As she attempted to put the scrawny baby to her breast tears filled her eyes.

The baby was too weak to suck so Maria expressed milk into its mouth. The baby swallowed the milk so Maria continued like this until the infant fell asleep.

Maria's tear-stained face looked up at Minas. "Tell me," she said.

Minas told Maria how he went back to the cave where they had left Stavros and Soula but found only Soula with her baby. Stavros had left her the first night after they heard screaming coming from below but he had never returned. The donkey had run away and she had only a little bread and cheese which she ate the next day. Then her pains intensified and she gave birth alone. The baby, whom she called Kalliopi (Poppy), was fine but Soula had lost a lot of blood. She fed the baby but with no nourishment for herself she became very weak. When Minas found her she could barely speak, had a fever and was dying.

"I stayed with her until she died."

But what happened to my brother Stavros?"

"I don't know; I think he is probably dead."

Maria's tears fell onto the tiny baby who slept in her arms. She cried for her brother Stavros, her sister-in-law Soula and the two little orphaned girls Eleni and Kalliopi who would now be their responsibility. The baby made a pitiful cry. Maria looked down at her as she offered her breast again but still the baby was too weak to suckle. Maria continued to express milk into the tiny mouth every time the infant woke during the night. By daybreak the baby was able to latch on to Maria's breast and fed a little before falling into an exhausted sleep.

"Thankfully you still have plenty of milk," said Minas, "otherwise the baby would have no chance of surviving."

"Yes, and I will do my best to help this little girl live but she is lethargic and far from well," Maria said as she took off her petticoat and tore it up to wrap around the baby.

The children were amazed to find a baby had arrived during the night and it helped to soothe their restlessness. Tiny Kalliopi was in Maria's arms all the time and little Christos was not very happy about his breasts being shared with this funny little thing that mewed like a kitten. Poor little Eleni missed her parents and asked for them constantly. She cried every night because she was accustomed to going to sleep with her mother singing to her. Minas and Maria were unsure what to tell Eleni about her parents.

Maria wanted to say they were in heaven and that she would meet them again one day. Minas was so angry with God that he forbade Maria to say anything about heaven or their religion. He insisted that the Kasiots were good God-fearing people who had been forsaken by their God. The couple decided not to tell the children anything for the moment, it was too much for them to cope with and if they told the children they would have to confront and cope with their own grief as well.

Sleeping was easy for the children but Minas and Maria found it difficult, never feeling completely safe in the cave. Minas decided that for their safety they should sleep further inside but discovered bats which disturbed them even more and also were known to carry diseases. So most nights at least one of them was usually awake for a good part of the night.

One night Minas dozed off and was woken suddenly by a high-pitched scream. He stumbled to his feet and tried to reach the opening to the cave but his legs kept giving way and he had to crawl. What he saw when he reached daylight caused him to cry out in anguish. His two little boys were being carried off under the arms of a huge man bare to the waist holding a large knife between his teeth. Then he saw Maria holding the baby being thrown onto the ground; the baby fell from her arms and began to roll down the mountainside. Minas tried to call her name but no sound came out and he was on his knees again crawling and falling. He made one last attempt to call Maria and as he did so got to his feet.

"What are you doing Minas, are you dreaming?" Maria stood and tried to comfort him.

"Oh Maria, I have just had the worst nightmare; it was horrible, just horrible."

"What did you dream?"

"No, it's too awful, I cannot tell you."

Maria held him in her arms and tried to soothe him as she would a child. "Shh, shh," she said. "You are awake now, it was only a dream."

Minas shook and took quite a while to calm down. "Yes that was only a dream but the whole thing is a nightmare, one that I wish we could wake from."

The nervous little family stayed in their hiding place for about a month and became tired of eating figs and tomatoes. Although they were aware of the other groups of people they kept to themselves most of the time. Only the men got together every few days to discuss the situation and all agreed to stay put and keep out of sight. One family appeared from over the other side of the island. They had been out fishing and happened to be returning to shore late on the day the enemy ships landed and were able to escape back to the safety of the sea. Landing their boat in an uninhabited part of the island they then climbed the mountain and found shelter.

Early one morning they woke to the smell of smoke and, looking down towards the port, Minas saw there were large fires burning in some of the villages. He decided it would be safe to kill and roast a goat inside the cave so they ate a good hot meal at last. Several days after this the last ship sailed out of the harbour and Minas, along with the other men, thought it might be safe to go home. Two of the men went down at night to see if it was safe and returned confirming the ships and the sailors had all departed.

The day Minas and Maria decided to go down they were very cautious. Minas led the way leading the goats, Christos rode the donkey and Maria followed with the other children. As they drew closer to their village they became aware of the absolute devastation that had taken place on the island.

The ground was scorched, crops were burnt, houses were burnt, some still half standing. Very few animals were visible, just a few cats and the odd chicken that had escaped the pillage. Most of the ships and fishing boats were damaged or sunk and the churches had been ransacked. A few people wandered around visibly distressed. As they passed through the upper area of their village they came across an old woman sitting in a damaged building crying "Yianni mou, Yianni mou [My John, my John]." Minas gently took her by the hand and asked her to come with them. "We will help you find Yianni," he said. She went with them and continued to wail and call for her Yianni. They returned to their home — or what was left of it. Two walls were partly standing, half the roof, a few pots, a tripod to put over a fire and a crucifix. Minas cleared out an area for them to stay in and found several of their chickens roosting in the broken rafters. He took one of their remaining pots to rinse out and brought it back filled with water then he made a small stone circle and started a little fire so that Maria could cook soup with the vegetables they had brought back. The sad old woman, who was unable to tell them her name and in fact did not even acknowledge them, sat in a corner moaning and rocking back and forth.

"I must go out to find out what I can, I will return as soon as I have some answers," Minas said. "Please don't go anywhere, and keep the children with you." As Minas went out he glanced behind him at his little family huddled together in the wreck of his home and felt real fear and loathing for the people responsible for the devastation and misery that surrounded them. He noticed as he walked evidence of the barbarism that had befallen his fellow islanders. There were many areas where blood stains were evident on the paths and roadways and parts of decomposing animal carcasses had been thrown into the bushes. Tears filled his eyes as he walked down the narrow pathway between the remaining ruined buildings.

Maria made the soup and fed the children, and offered some to the wailing woman. "Come Kyria, [Mrs] you must eat something," said Maria, but the poor woman did not respond; she was so distressed it was as if she was in a trance and she continued to rock back and forth.

The family sat quietly waiting for Minas to return, George on one side of Maria, Eleni sitting on the other side, little Christos on her knee and baby Kalliopi balanced above Christos sucking hungrily on Maria's breast. Maria had said nothing to the children about the devastation that surrounded them but she did not have to, they could see for themselves and they knew it was very bad.

When Minas returned he brought with him a blanket, a few bits and pieces for the kitchen and a big bucket of clean water. Maria washed the children and made a bed for them in the corner of the wrecked house. Minas waited for her to sit down before he told her what he had discovered.

**

The Wailing Woman

Yianni mou, Yianni mou, oh my god what has happened?
Is this hell?
Where is god?
Why did they kill Yianni?
Why have they killed so many?
Why have they taken my grandchildren on to that ship?
Why have they burnt the church?
Why did they violate the women and girls?
Who are these people and what have we done to them?
God where are you? I want to die.

**

14

Massacre

Minas had met up with other likeminded men who were seeking answers and wanting to assist the few remaining islanders. Between them they agreed to join together and house everyone in close proximity and to share food and cooking to ensure no one starved. It was also decided to document everything that had happened and to count the remaining islanders. Minas discovered that thousands of people had been slaughtered and only a few old people had been spared. Young boys and girls had been rounded up and taken on to the ships. Priests had been killed trying to protect their churches; animals had been slaughtered and eaten or taken by the soldiers. The few people who had survived had been, like themselves, up in the mountains or able to hide somehow.

"But who are these devils who hate us so much and why would they want to destroy the lives of peaceful hard-working people?" cried Maria.

"I am not sure but I think they could be Egyptians under orders of the Turks. Why they have done this dreadful thing I do not know," said Minas.

"Are you sure they have killed so many people? Where are the bodies?"

"There is evidence that they've dug huge graves – probably to hide what they have done, not out of any goodness."

Maria cried bitterly at the thought of what had happened to her fellow islanders and in particular the children who had been taken. Although she knew the children's lives would not be pleasant she was too naive to imagine what dreadful things might be done to them. Minas was not so naive: he knew that the children would be used as slaves, sold, raped and most would lose their identity, their culture, their religion and many their lives.

"Someone has put the evil eye on us!" Maria cried.

"Do not say such silly things," said Minas.

"Well why has God allowed this to happen to us?" she said.

"What god?" uttered Minas harshly.

Some people had lived very high up in the mountains and these people were mainly spared. In most of the villages some houses had been destroyed but others were undamaged therefore everyone could be housed. If families wanted to move to an undamaged house permanently or until they repaired their own dwelling they could. The small group of self-appointed leaders along with the priests tried to maintain order and requested that people only take what they needed from an empty house, but some looting and raiding did take place.

For centuries Kasos had been a prosperous democratic island of ship builders and experienced sea-farers. They owned a large fleet of ships and took part in trade with countries near and far. This brought considerable wealth to the island which enabled independence and contentment for the eleven thousand inhabitants of Kasos.

They were under Turkish rule and when the Greeks began an uprising against the governing Ottomans in 1821, the whole of the Kasiot fleet was involved. Mehmet Ali, the Turkish governor of Egypt, considered the fleet an impediment to his plan to take over Crete. His intention was to attack the Peloponnese from a base on Crete and stop the uprising.

It was because Mehmet Ali feared the highly capable Kasiot fleet would thwart his attack that he sent the Ottoman-Egyptian navy to Kasos to slaughter the people. They killed around 7000 people and took many young boys and girls on to their boats. The only inhabitants to survive were those who lived very high up in a mountain village, those who were able to hide in the mountains or those who were not on the island at the time.

/5

Surviving

Over the next weeks and months the traumatised islanders struggled with day to day life. Some lost the will to live while others banded together to help each other survive but it was a very difficult time as they were all heartbroken. The strange woman that Maria and Minas had brought home with them would not eat and never told them her name: the only words she uttered were Yanni mou, Yanni mou. One morning they found the poor woman had died in her sleep; Maria said she had died of a broken heart.

There was still food up in the mountains including rabbits and herds of free-ranging goats as well as plenty of fish in the sea. So it was not a lack of food that made life difficult – it was a general depression that was felt by them all. Some said it was like having a stone in the heart or a large burden on their back that they were unable to put down. It was only the strongest who could cope with the aftermath of the massacre and soon people began to talk of leaving the island.

Nearby on the island of Karpathos the population soon heard of the massacre and their priests urged the people to open their hearts and their homes to help the unfortunate people of Kasos. Then further afield on Crete the same invitations were offered.

"I think we should go to Crete," said Minas. "We are young and we can rebuild our lives, and the children will be better off in a larger community."

"Yes," Maria agreed." I don't want to leave our island but I know it will be better for us and mostly for the children."

So like many others they began to make plans to leave. Damaged boats had to be hauled out of the water and the timber dried off to repair any craft worth salvaging. The large trees on the island had been depleted by a long history of ship building and most of the remaining trees had been burnt by the invaders. Tools had to be reclaimed from the ashes and as some of the best ship builders had been slaughtered, the repair work took much longer than would otherwise have been the case.

It was prudent to go before winter came because the sea would become rougher and they did not want to risk any more catastrophes. As the people became ready to depart boats began to leave frequently, usually in small groups. They set out early in the morning knowing that the trip could take several days. The morning Minas and Maria left was in October so the weather was still fine. The boat was packed with their few belongings which included chickens and goats from which they hoped to breed. The children were excited, Maria was sad.

"Look back at Kasos, Maria, you may never see it again," said Minas.

"No," said Maria, tears streaming down her cheeks, "I don't want to see Kasos; I will try to remember it as it used to be, not as it is now."

16

Leaving Kasos

Minas and Maria began their new life on the island of Crete in the village of Sitia. The house they were allotted was much smaller than they were used to but they felt safe again. Minas began fishing as soon as they were settled because he had to pay a small rent after one month as well as keep his family.

Maria kept her goats in a little makeshift pen just outside the door. She had to tie their front and back legs together so they would not stray. Normally she would not do this but she could not afford to lose even one goat otherwise her plans to begin cheese making in the future would be futile.

Gradually the children were told what had happened. Eleni had sensed something awful had befallen her parents and was very protective of her little sister Kalliopi. She helped to care for her and played games and sang clapping songs with her.

Kalliopi thrived on Maria's milk and smiled at everyone, blissfully unaware of the awful circumstances of her birth. The children played with other children from the village and Maria made friends with the women she met at church and the marketplace.

George was also very protective of little Kalliopi who he remembered coming into their lives on that night up on the mountain. He took special care of her and she became very close to him. Their lives were as good as they could be and gradually they began to think less of the massacre and their ravaged island and more of the future.

Maria and Minas never thought of the two girls as their nieces and as the children looked alike, it was never mentioned to anyone. Maria devoted herself to the four children, always aware that the trauma they had all been through could affect them at any stage. She was patient and loving, at all times putting the needs of the children before anything else. She took them to church and told them stories of the saints they were named after and celebrated their name days. She also taught them to cook Kasiot foods, which she had been taught by her mother. She made up nice stories with happy endings to keep them positive and sang Kasiot folk songs to them so they could have fun together. There was even a little bit of dancing to her tunes.

17

George returns to Kasos, 1840

Minas and Maria and others of their age never fully recovered their peace of mind or regained their status in the community but the children, who had been too young to remember the horror, were more optimistic and coped better. As they grew into their teens and early adulthood some began to talk of returning to Kasos as the families all had farmland, property or houses which they could repair or rebuild.

George was one of the young men who thought of going back and he discussed it with Minas and Maria. Of course they didn't want him to go but he persisted and eventually they gave him their blessing to give it a go.

George returned to Kasos as a twenty-year-old along with others who wanted to make their lives there. It was not easy but George gradually rebuilt his parents' home and fenced in a small plot where the family had once kept three or four goats. He fished for himself and traded with other islanders for yogurt and other basics. There was now a baker in his village to buy bread from and when the women took their pots to the bakery to cook in the large oven he sometimes traded fish for a meal of moussaka or something else delicious from the oven.

After a year of hard work he returned to Crete to see his family. The family did not know he was coming so they were very surprised and happy to see him. George was shocked to find Eleni was married and expecting a baby but his biggest surprise was how Kalliopi had changed in the short time he had been away. She was sixteen and had grown into a beautiful young woman. Her large brown eyes and shy, pretty smile stunned George.

"She is beautiful," said George to his mother.

"Yes and there are two young men who have begun to pay attention to her," she replied.

George was surprised at his feeling of alarm when he heard that.

He spoke to Kalliopi about her future with one of these men and she said she was not keen to leave the family at the moment and she did not want to marry either of the men.

George was relieved to hear this and went back to Kasos confident she would be with Minas and Maria when he visited again.

18

George in Kasos

Life on Kasos was not easy for George but he became an integral part of the community, giving help and support to others who returned to the island. There were goats and donkeys which had been left on the island to be caught and claimed. Simple vegetables were grown and local herbs were sourced. There was an abundance of rabbits for anyone to trap and fishermen continued to take their boats out to catch the loved seafood of the local waters. George never forgot the conversation he had had with Kalliopi before he left and he could not get the image of her shy smile and quiet manner out of his mind. After two years he decided to revisit his parents in Sitia on Crete.

They were extremely pleased to see him and he was surprised that now his younger brother Christos was married to a woman called Vera and that Eleni had given birth to a second baby.

When George entered the house he looked around and said, "Where is Kalliopi?"

"She will be here soon, she helps Eleni with her children each day," replied his mother.

When Kalliopi walked through the door she stopped sharply at the sight of George before running into his arms and kissing him. The kiss changed from one of welcome to one of passion. Without their mother noticing they drew apart and looked at each other with shocked surprise.

As Kalliopi helped Maria with food preparation for the evening meal she was aware of a strange feeling brought on by George's presence. It was difficult for her to concentrate on her tasks and at the dinner table she could not look him in the eye without blushing. George was a man now and his body was fit and masculine and when he looked at Kalliopi his amber eyes aroused a feeling previously unknown to her. It was a wonderful feeling but troublesome too because of its unfamiliarity. She felt a little breathless and her heart seemed to beat too fast and every time he came near her she blushed and felt a rush of something hot and intense inside her body.

After dinner had been eaten and Kalliopi had helped her mother clean up the kitchen, George spoke to his mother. "I am going to walk down to the port to check on my boat, can Kalliopi walk with me?"

"Of course she can. The fresh air in the evening is very good for you."

It was a beautiful evening, warm and mild, as they began to walk. There were noisy cicadas and rabbits ran and jumped in the scrub but George and Kalliopi were oblivious to everything except each other. They had not touched again since that afternoon but both were wanting to and at the same time felt that they should not.

"Kalliopi, I have missed you so much and you have been on my mind constantly since I left," said George.

"And I have thought of you all that time," she answered.

They stopped walking and turned to face each other. George put out his hand and pulled Kalliopi towards him. "I love you Kalliopi."

"I love you also."

"Will you marry me, Kalliopi?" George asked as he put both his arms around her.

"Can we marry?"

"We are not brother and sister so we can," he said.

"People will talk, everyone in Sitia thinks we are brother and sister."

"We won't be living in Sitia, we will be in Kasos," said George and he stooped to kiss Kalliopi on the lips.

They walked to the port and checked the boat then walked slowly back to the house, stopping frequently to kiss in the dark.

When they returned George told his parents of their desire to marry. Both Minas and Maria were doubtful but at the same time understanding. Maria suggested they should speak to the local priest as soon as possible. Later that night the young couple crept outside to be in each other's arms again and to talk about their future together. Each night Kalliopi walked with George to the port to check on his boat and each night they would sit outside in the dark to be alone. One night they found the attraction between them magnified by the strong moonlight as it edged over the top of the mountain. Neither of them had any experience with the opposite sex but nature took over and they could not stay apart, both were swept along by desire and love. Their bodies were ripe for love making and it seemed the most natural thing to do – as it was, and from that night they knew they had to be together no matter what.

Several days later they went to see the priest to discuss their marriage. But although the priest said he was sorry, he said he would not marry them because they were brother and sister.

"No," said George, "We are not brother and sister, we are cousins."

"Still I cannot marry you: first cousins cannot marry either. I am deeply sorry but it is not allowed."

He would not be persuaded. They went away devastated. Minas went also to speak to the priest but to no avail, he would not budge on his decision.

Manoli, one of the men who had been pursuing Kalliopi, heard that the priest had refused to marry the couple and visited Minas and Maria again asking for Kalliopi.

George was present when he called and he was very angry and upset.

"She does not want to marry you," said George. "Get out of this house and don't come back."

George and Kalliopi were very much in love and would not be deterred. After much talking and arguing with Minas and Maria they decided the only way they could be together was to elope to Kasos and hopefully marry there. Plans were made to leave secretly early one morning and in the preceding days they took various items belonging to Kalliopi to George's boat. Kalliopi wrote a letter to Minas and Maria telling them of her wish to be George's wife and that eloping was the only way that could be achieved. Unfortunately on the morning they set off for the boat they were stopped by Manoli who had been watching them and had worked out what they were doing. He approached the couple and spoke to Kalliopi.

"Kalliopi you are making a mistake, stay here and be my wife. I own several boats, you will have your own house, and you won't have to work at all. What does this poor man have to offer you?"

Kalliopi stayed calm and thanked Manoli but insisted she wanted to be with George. George on the other hand was enraged and turned his large frame to stand over the man.

"Get out of my way, leave us alone, we are going and you will not stop us," he said angrily.

Manoli in desperation pushed George towards the edge of the port hoping to push him into the sea. George grabbed at Manoli to stop himself from falling, causing Manoli to fall and hit his head.

The couple boarded the boat and sailed off.

19

George and Kalliopi in Kasos

As they sailed Kalliopi and George discussed Manoli, hoping that he had not suffered a serious injury. From the boat as it moved into the waves they could not see if he had got to his feet or not.

"What if he is dead, we can never return now," Kalliopi cried.

"I am sure he is not badly hurt," said George hopefully.

As soon as Kalliopi set foot on Kasos she felt at ease and began to turn their humble house into a home. George had made simple furniture and Kalliopi had brought some curtains she had sewn and a cover for the bed which she had embroidered. There were always wildflowers in a vase on the windowsill and tasty food ready for George when he returned from a hard day's work. They were very happy together and so much in love. Kalliopi reasoned that if God had made it possible to love another person as she loved George and for them to give so much pleasure to each other then it must be a good thing.

Kalliopi loved the island from the first day she set foot on the shore. Often she would waste time gazing up at the high brown mountains watching the remaining windmill blades turning in the wind. Sometimes she watched the hawks swooping and calling to their fledglings to leave the nest and fly with them. At night she loved to spot the small owls which hunted for mice outside their house.

They never approached the priest about getting married because shortly after they arrived on the island Kalliopi realised that she was pregnant.

The shame of admitting that they had been intimate before marriage was too much so they decided to pretend that the wedding had taken place in Crete.

Kalliopi had had the name Mavrikakis since she had been taken care of by Minas and Maria so that was not a problem and they decided in the beginning to keep to themselves so that they could avoid questions and not have to tell lies.

"God will understand won't he?" asked Kalliopi. "He knows what is in our hearts."

"Maybe God will, but not the people and particularly not the priests."

Kalliopi began to breed goats in the hope that soon she would have enough to start making cheese as her mother had taught her which she could sell. She tended a small vegetable garden at the front of the house and a few chickens scratched about and laid plenty of eggs. Her pregnancy progressed without any trouble and they were happy together. George made a cradle and Kalliopi sewed tiny baby clothes for the baby.

In the first year on Kasos, Kalliopi gave birth to a sickly baby girl who from the moment of birth was very pale with bluish lips and fingers. The baby, whom they named Maria, lived only a few days, never strong enough to feed for long, barely able to cry and always struggling to breathe. After she died Kalliopi wrapped her in a blanket and sat crying and rocking her for a whole day. Eventually she passed the tiny body to George and said, "We have committed a great sin and God has punished us for not being married."

"No Kalliopi, it happens sometimes; the poor baby was not strong enough to live. We will have more babies," said George. "You will see, give it time."

"Do you think God will allow our baby to go to heaven?"

"Yes. I am sure God will allow our baby into heaven and will not let any more bad luck come to you or me. You can wear the Mati* if that will make you feel better."

Kalliopi regained her health and happiness and busied herself with everyday life and eventually gave birth to two more children a boy (Minas) and a girl (Soula) who both grew into happy, healthy children with no sign of the illness that had ended their infant sister's life.

---

*Mati – a blue glass eye worn to ward off bad luck or evil,
if you believe someone has put the evil eye on you.

George and Kalliopi did not ever return to Crete for two reasons: they could not face Minas' and Maria's questions about their marriage and they were uncertain of Manoli's fate. This caused a great deal of anguish to both of them but they reasoned that had Manoli died they probably would have been informed, though they could not be sure. As for not seeing their parents again, that was a sacrifice they had made when deciding to elope and now they had to live with the consequences.

20

Filos

From a young age Minas helped his father George to repair their boat, to untangle and repair the nets used for fishing and, when he was old enough and could swim, he was allowed to go out in the boat to fish with his father. On one particular day at sea they returned to shore and their usual site to clean the catch where the sea birds were always waiting for a free meal from the fishermen. The men threw the scraps into the sea or up in the air and the birds squawked and screeched in an effort to get to the food first. On this day there was an injured pelican which had a limp and a broken wing. It was shunned by the other pelicans so Minas felt sorry for it and kept fish scraps just for him. After that the pelican became attached to Minas and waited for him at the shore when he went out in the boat. It was not long before the pelican that they called Filos began to follow Minas everywhere he went. It was a common sight to see Minas and the pelican at the beach or in the streets or watching Minas as he played with the other children. Filos followed Minas right up to the front door of their house but Kalliopi would not let him in.

"He can sleep with the chickens, they are cousins after all," she said.

"But he cannot fly and he might need me to protect him at night," said Minas.

"He was okay without you before, I am sure he will be safe with the chickens at night."

Minas was eventually happy with this arrangement and found Filos waiting for him at the door of the chicken coop each morning. Filos became his best friend and Minas chattered away to the pelican as if he understood Greek. Minas became known as 'bird boy', a name he quite liked because he was developing an interest in all the sea birds and other birds of the island. He knew how long the parents sat on their eggs during springtime and when the hawk fledglings were ready to leave the nest. He paid close attention to how many days the chicks spent on the edge of the nest or on a tree branch before they took their first flight. As he got older he knew exactly where the nests were and how many chicks could survive and how many days before they became independent. He wrote all this information in a book with detailed drawings and bird feathers that he picked up when observing.

Minas showed his father who was impressed with what his son had done and surprised at the sketches of birds, which had been very well drawn. He took the book to Kalliopi to see and she was also proud of her son's ability even if to her it seemed useless information.

"It's not really useful information Minas," George reflected to his son.

"I know, but it is very interesting and I've written down all that I have learned about the birds."

As Minas grew up his pelican friend Filos was always nearby or waiting at the port until one day when Minas and his father George returned from fishing he was nowhere to be seen.

"He must be sick or hurt because he has never missed welcoming us home for years," said Minas.

"Yes that's true," said his father, "We will ask around. Someone must have seen him."

They did ask and were told that two boys had been seen with Filos earlier that day.

"Who are they?" asked Minas. "Where did they take him?"

"I don't know but they had a string around his neck and were leading him away from the port."

No one was able to identify the boys or say where they had taken the pelican. Minas was very upset and began searching for his beloved pet before going home. It was well and truly dark when he finally went home without finding Filos. He could not sleep and tossed and turned most of the night, rising as soon as the sun began to light the sky. Without eating breakfast and ignoring his mother calling for him to come back, he headed off to search for Filos. He did not find him and went home feeling very unhappy. As he entered the kitchen his parents exchanged glances which he observed and asked, "What have you heard? Have you found him? Has anyone seen him?"

"Sit down Minas," said his father. "I have bad news for you about Filos. He has been found floating in the sea and he is dead."

"Why, what happened to him?" cried Minas.

George knew he had to tell his son the truth because in such a small village someone else would tell if he did not.

"Those boys were very cruel to him and they hung him in a tree."

"Why?" Minas began to sob. "Why would anyone want to hurt a beautiful defenceless bird?"

"Minas, I don't know why people do such things but it has happened and we can't change that."

"I want to find those boys and speak to them," said Minas, trying to regain his composure.

"Yes we will find out who they are and we will speak to them," said his father.

Several days later when George and Minas returned from fishing Kalliopi had news for them about the boys who had taken Filos. She told them they were from another village and the name of the family. After dinner George and Minas set off to find the family with the intention of speaking to the boys. Arriving at the edge of the village they asked the way to the family home and had to walk through the village and further up the mountain to find it. There were two barking dogs tied up outside the dwelling which was no better than an outhouse fit for animals and the two boys were actually in a goat enclosure with the goats.

"This does not look good," said George. "We had better take care."

They avoided the house and walked over to the boys who appeared to be preparing to bed down for the night. George spoke to them.

"Yiassas Pethia [hello boys]. We are looking for two boys about your age who took our pet pelican, do you know where we can find them?"

The two grubby boys, who were dressed in filthy ragged clothes, looked at each other and then at George; the smaller one began to cry.

"Well?" demanded Minas.

The older boy began to shake and said, "Please don't hurt us, we didn't mean to kill the pelican."

"He was my friend," said Minas. "He has been with me since I was very young. I miss him."

Both the boys were crying now and the older one began to tell what had happened between sobs and hiccups. He described how they had seen Minas with the bird and asked their father if they could have a pelican too. Their father had said the pelican was a free bird and did not belong to anyone so if they wanted it they only had to lead it away and it could be theirs. When they took it home the dogs barked at it and it was scared. The boys were worried that if the dogs were off the leash they would harm the frightened pelican. Their father had said, "it's a bird isn't it, put it in a tree then the dogs will not get it". So they tried to secure it with the string in a tree to keep it safe and decided they would return it the next day rather than see it killed. When they woke the next morning the pelican was hanging by the neck over a branch and the dogs were pulling and tugging at the carcass.

Just as the crying boy finished telling the sad tale his father emerged from the dwelling and began to yell at George and Minas to go away.

"What are you doing here? Get off my land and leave my poor motherless boys alone!"

"He is drunk," Minas murmured to his father.

George turned to look at the man, "Endaxie, endaxie [okay, okay], we are just having an evening stroll; we have never been up here before, just having a look around," and to Minas he said, "We can't improve things by taking this any further. It's clear the boys were badly advised by their father and are very upset at what has happened. If they are motherless we don't want to make their lives any more miserable if we can help it. I wouldn't be surprised if he hurt them if we made trouble. I will have a word with the local priest and see what we can do for them."

Minas did not say anything but thought about how kind and understanding his father was and so different to the father of the two unfortunate boys who had been responsible for the death of his beloved pet.

Back at home Kalliopi was waiting patiently to hear what had happened and was touched by the sad plight of the two boys.

"Do you still have some clothes that Minas has outgrown?" George asked her. "I think those two boys could do with some new clothes."

"Yes, I will get them for you."

"Good, I will take them to the priest and he can give them to the boys." Minas took it all in and looked at his parents with love and admiration. His family were not well off but they always thought of others. He was still upset about Filos but understood why his father had decided not to tell the boys' father he was the owner of the pelican; he knew it would not ease his pain and it would probably cause more pain to the two unfortunate boys.

**

Pelican Abductors

My brother and I are very poor and we do not go to school. Pa forces us to look after the goats and the chickens and we sleep with the goats. We are smelly and dirty and no one likes us.

Pa is drunk every afternoon and sometimes he beats us. We don't have a mother, she died a few years ago having a baby, that's when Pa went a bit strange. My brother is my only friend. When we saw the pelican we were envious but we did not think we could have it. Pa said it was a free bird and that it belonged to no one. He said we could take it so we did. We thought it might be wrong to take it and it was wrong. The men who came looking for the pelican were sad, we thought they would beat us but they were kind. Now we are very sorry.

**

Over the next half century the people who lived on Kasos were at the mercy of the sea and the sky. If they had a wet winter the island would flourish but dry winters wreaked havoc on them, making it difficult to farm the land. Likewise if the sea was too rough, as it was at times, it was dangerous to go out and risk life even though the fishermen of Kasos had been great seamen.

The population was small and the massacre had a lasting effect on the morale and confidence of the people.

2 /

Minas marries Theone, circa 1854

When Minas was in his early twenties he married Theone who was from his village. Theone shared his love of birds and they often walked on the cliffs and the mountains searching and watching the island birds. When Minas showed Theone his book of bird sketches and information she was amazed at his realistic illustrations and encouraged him to do more. He added to the book by drawing other things such as wildflowers, bees and little animals. The book took pride of place in the rustic home Theone created for them.

Two years into their marriage Theone gave birth to twin boys, George and Nicholas. George was born first and was the bigger of the two; Nicholas was very small and weak and not well enough to survive. In spite of Theone's efforts to feed him and keep him warm and her prayers to God, the little baby died. It was a very sad time for the couple but thankfully George thrived. Baby George became the centre of attention for the young couple as no other babies were born. Almost every day he would sit on his mother's knee and look at his father's illustrated book of birds and animals. He loved his father's book and called it 'Biblio-Papa' (Papa's book).

When George was a small boy he liked to help his mother in the kitchen as she cooked each day. Theone was happy to have him by her side and he would act as a little helper, picking up the eggs from the chickens, counting out onions or choosing the biggest piece of garlic for his mother. On one such day one of the neighbours yelled for Theone and she went to the door to see what the fuss was about. Little George remained in the kitchen and decided to continue what his mother had been doing. The stew simmered in a large pot and on the bench beside the fire was a handful of chopped herbs which George knew his mother would put into the stew. He decided to do it for her so he reached for the herbs and attempted to place them in the pot. The pot was too high for him and too hot to touch so that when his little fingers felt the hot metal he pulled back suddenly, causing the pot to spill all over the right side of his face and upper body. George screamed and Theone came running back inside.

"Yiorgi mou, Yiorgi mou, [my George] what have you done?"

The child continued to scream and his skin turned bright red. Theone called to her neighbour who had heard the commotion and was hurrying in.

"Maria help me, my boy has spilt the stew and is burnt!"

"Do you have butter?" asked Maria.

"No I have nothing like that, what should I do?"

"We will take him to the sea then, it's the only thing I can think of."

The two women rushed the poor child down to the shore and Theone sat in the water with George on her knee, trying to cool his burning flesh. With her hand she ladled the cool sea water over his face and shoulders as she cried bitter tears that fell onto his wavy black hair.

George was extremely sick and sore for a long time and as his burns began to heal he developed terrible scars. Every time his mother looked at him she would relive the awful moments of the accident. She felt responsible and wondered why God was punishing them. When Minas walked through the door one day he found his wife wailing and she began to lament, "God is punishing us but for what? What have we done to deserve this?

"I don't think so," said Minas. "Surely God cannot keep an eye on all the people in the world. Besides we have done nothing wrong."

"Well if it is not us, someone else in the family must have done something in the past and we are paying for it now. I think we should speak to the priest and ask for a special blessing otherwise we will keep having bad luck."

"If it will make you feel better," said Minas "but we have to concentrate on George now and help him to survive this awful accident."

As Minas uttered these words he looked at his wife who was guilt-ridden and worn out with lack of sleep and his heart broke for her. He accompanied her to see their priest who said a special prayer for them and Theone felt some relief and hope for the future.

George did survive but with thick ugly scars that marred his otherwise beautiful face and attracted attention whenever he went out. This caused him to become self-conscious and withdrawn and he spent more time at home with his mother than with other children. He was happy in his mother's company when he was young because she taught him children's songs and told him stories, which he loved. His favourites were the fables by Aesop, in particular one about a fox and a crow.

THE FOX AND THE CROW

A crow once stole a piece of cheese from a house and flew up into a tree. He was just about to start eating the cheese when along came a fox. Knowing his only hope of getting the cheese was to get the crow to open his beak he began to flatter the crow. The fox told the crow that he was a fine-looking bird with beautiful shining feathers.

No one had ever said such nice things to the crow so he was very pleased. But he still had the cheese in his beak. The fox said to him that he wondered if his voice was as beautiful as his appearance and if so he must be the most favoured of all the birds. This was too much for the crow and he opened his beak and began to sing. The cheese fell to the ground and the fox gobbled it up and ran off laughing at how clever he was.

Every time Theone told this story to little George he hoped that the crow would not drop the cheese but his mother stuck to the story and the cheese always ended up being eaten by the fox.

"But Mummy surely the crow has learnt by now that the fox only wants the cheese," said George.

Theone laughed at her boy saying, "That is the way the story goes. Maybe when you grow up you can write another one with a different ending."

Sometimes for a treat Minas sat with George on his knee and made up stories with the aid of his Biblio-Papa.

As George got older he began to go out in the boat with his father and he was content to do this as no one could see his face. He learned to read the sea, the sky and the wind with regard to fishing and safety on the sea and became a promising seaman at quite a young age.

When George was about ten years old Theone gave birth to identical twin girls Kalliopi and Aphrodite. They were like two peas in a pod — huge brown eyes, chubby cheeks, thick dark curls and smiles to melt even the hardest heart. Kalliopi and Aphro (for short) cured their mother's misgivings about God punishing them as she now felt very blessed with her family. The little girls loved their big brother and George adored them. He read to them, took them for walks, taught them to collect the eggs and sometimes carried them on his back pretending to be a donkey, but one thing the girls were not allowed to do was help in the kitchen. The fear of having another child burnt was too awful to contemplate and Theone would not take any chances.

"Not until you are tall enough to see everything at the same level as I do," said Theone. "Then you will learn to cook in the kitchen with me."

So the girls learned to tend the garden, watering and pulling up weeds, and feed the chickens and house goats. When one of the hens became broody and sat on the eggs for three weeks the little girls would lift the hen daily to see if the chicks had hatched and when they did, they squealed with delight and carefully carried the tiny chicks inside to show their mother. They were a happy family even if it was often a hand to mouth existence, supplemented by the little vegetable garden and the few chickens scratching around in the yard.

As George approached adulthood he felt a strong urge to be married. His cousin Soula had wed at age sixteen and he witnessed her blooming with the advent of matrimony and motherhood. He noticed the pretty village girls but was too shy to look directly into their eyes, but if he had he would have seen that they were accustomed to his scars and did not think they were such a bad thing as he did. Out at sea with his father he brought up the subject of his future, thinking he would be a lonely man who would never marry or have a family of his own.

"Oh George, certainly you will marry some day, if a woman loves you she won't even see the scars."

"Do you really mean that Pa? How will I meet this woman?"

"From now on you must lift your eyes up and cast around until you catch the eye of someone who you like the look of. If she is giving you a similar look smile at her. If she smiles back, next time you see her, smile again and say hello."

"Is that all?"

"It may be enough but you tell me who she is and I will speak to her parents."

George was pleased to hear these words of wisdom from his father and gave it a lot of thought. He decided that at the next festival to be celebrated he would go as usual but instead of staying in the kitchen with his mother and helping with the food he would try to spend more time outside. When the bread was blessed by the priest he offered to take the basket of sliced bread around to the folk who had come to the church to celebrate. People thanked him and smiled and he was surprised that no one seemed to mind his scars. George gained a lot of confidence from this first day out and he began to go out more on his own to the village square and the kaffenion where the men sat and drank coffee in the sunshine. This was where they congregated when they had spare time to talk and pass on local gossip or discuss Greek politics. He became one of the regulars and was greeted warmly by the men when he approached.

During this time George had been looking shyly at local girls but although there were many attractive faces he had not noticed one who really took his fancy and he thought to himself, "They are nice to look at but what are they really like? If I am going to marry a girl just because she is pretty, will she be someone I can talk to and share my thoughts with?"

One day George was sitting alone at the kaffenion and he overheard a man speaking quietly to his companion about his youngest daughter.

"I don't know what will become of my girl Chrisoula, she is a plain little thing but she is very clever and I know she would like to marry but some men do not like a woman who has opinions and ideas. I worry that she will not marry and I know it is something she wants very much."

"Does she have a suitor?"

"No, she says most of the young men are ignorant and she has nothing to say to them. We have suggested this one and that one but she refuses to meet them."

George pricked up his ears at this story and stole a glance at the man who was called Kosta. He had not known that he had a daughter and did not even know where he lived. That evening he asked his father about Kosta.

"Pa I heard a man called Kosta talking about his daughter Chrisoula; do you know who they are?"

"Yes I think so but ask your mother, she usually knows the girls by name."

Kalliopi had heard their conversation and said, "Yes I know that family and I know the girl, she is a very good girl who always has something interesting to say and helps out with the little children who do not go to school."

This was true. Chrisoula loved to teach the children things she had learnt from her parents who had both had only a little education. Most of the boys went to school for a few years but the girls were mostly educated at home. First she taught them songs and told stories. Aesop's fables were her favourites and the children also loved the stories because they were usually about animals and events they could relate to. She acquired some writing books and pencils for the children and they learned the alphabet and numbers. When the older girls were sitting in the sun doing their needlework or mending, Chrisoula would read to them and encourage them to read simple words and numbers from her books. She was surprised when her father told her of George's desire to meet her and agreed to an afternoon joint family gathering. She said she remembered George as the boy with the nice face who had a scar on his cheek.

The afternoon arrived and the two families met at the home of Minas and Theone. They drank coffee and ate sweet spoon-fruits which Theone had made. The young couple did not say much but both agreed afterwards that they would like to begin a courtship. Each weekend the families arranged for the couple to see each other for a few hours and eventually they left them alone briefly. During one of these brief meetings George asked Chrisoula to marry him and she replied, "I was thinking I would have to ask you myself if you did not ask me today."

George smiled and kissed her briefly on the lips, hoping her parents had not seen.

"You have made me very happy agapi mou [my love]."

George went home with the memory of the kiss on his mind well into the night. He hoped Chrisoula had enjoyed it as much as he had.

22

George and Chrisoula, circa 1900

Chrisoula had a new dress when she married George at the local church and Aphro and Kalliopi, who held candles for the marriage ceremony, wore new blue ribbons in their hair in an attempt to tame their thick dark curls. Everyone was happy and there was a party with music and dancing after a traditional Greek meal. Minas presented George and Chrisoula with the Biblio-Papa which was one of their most prized possessions. Chrisoula had not seen the book before and was enchanted by the realistic drawings and written information. Soon after they settled into their new home Chrisoula began to make a fabric cover for the book with embroidered birds and flowers on the border and needleworked:

BIBLIO-PAPA
by MINAS MAVRIKAKIS

in the centre of the cover.

Once again the book took pride of place in the household in which it was to be found.

Until Chrisoula gave birth to her own children she still managed to spend some time reading and teaching local children, and took great pride in housekeeping for George and herself. Aphro and Stasi joined in these sessions and offered to take over when Chrisoula was expecting her first baby. As it turned out she was telling the story of the fox and the crow when she felt her first pains which hit her like a hammer. Aphro and Stasi helped her home and went to bring her mother who arrived just in time to deliver the squealing baby boy. Aphro and Kalliopi cried with emotion as they watched Chrisoula put her baby to the breast where he began to suckle hungrily. They had forgotten about George, who walked through the door to find tears and laughter in equal abundance.

"What is all the noise about?" he asked.

"The baby came quickly," said his mother-in-law.

"Chrisoula, my love, are you all right?"

"I feel wonderful and I couldn't feel any happier." She smiled up at her husband who could not believe his eyes.

"I thought it would take all day!"

"Sometimes it does but not this time," she replied.

Theone rushed through the door with Minas hurrying behind her. "Has the baby come?" Theone cried.

"Yes," said George, "Meet baby Minas."

23

Minas and Katerina go to Egypt, circa 1900

Life on Kasos continued to be a struggle, nevertheless the small community slowly rebuilt its churches and established schools for the children. The buildings were whitewashed annually and most people began to see a brighter future. In spite of this Kasos was still poor and when the Suez Canal Company made it known that they wanted to employ experienced seamen, thousands of Kasiots left their island behind to resettle in Egypt. So by 1900 the population of Kasos had plummeted again while the Greek population of Egypt increased. In 1907 there were nearly 7000 Greeks living in Egypt.

The people lived and worked in towns along the Suez Canal such as Ismailia, Port Said and Suez. It was a great melting pot of Europeans from around the Mediterranean. Most Greeks learned to speak multiple languages as a consequence. There had been an organised community of Greeks living in Cairo since 1856 and the newcomers swelled the numbers by thousands. Greeks established their own communities with churches, schools and social clubs all living alongside French, English, Italian and Egyptian people.

Descendants of Minas and Maria Mavrikakis who had survived the terrible massacre on Kasos were among those who went to Egypt. They were Minas (son of George and Chrisoula Mavrikakis) and Katerina his wife. Minas, like his father and grandfather, was a fisherman and sometime carpenter and was employed repairing boats and marine fixtures. They lived in the cosmopolitan town of Ismailia which was once known as the "City of Beauty and Enchantment" because of its French-inspired architecture and beautiful parks and gardens. Minas and Katerina lived in a small house, one of many built by the Suez Canal Company for its employees. Life was good as the company paid a fair wage and looked after their workers. Minas worked on the boats as they piloted the large merchant ships that passed through the canal.

Their first son – another George – and one daughter, Dora, had been born in Kasos and two more daughters were born in Ismailia. The family were happy with their new life. The children went to school and church and played with the other children and led an idyllic life. They learned to swim and played in the shallows of the canal and were all as brown as berries. Sometimes they would catch fish and their mother would cook it for dinner. The climate was warm and fruit trees grew in abundance; heavily laden boughs of figs and mangos hung over fences free to anyone who wished to pick them – which George and his sisters often did. George was asked to sing in the church each Sunday which made his parents extremely proud. George was pleased with himself also until he realised he could never get out of going to church now or the priest would tell his parents.

As Easter approached, as usual there was to be a big celebration with a goat cooked on the spit and special bread baked to break their fast. As the children made their way home from school they were looking forward to the red dyed eggs they would have on Sunday to play the smashing egg game. Although they were fasting they were allowed to eat a small amount of fruit but not quite as much as they had done on the way home today.

"Just as well Pa is away until tomorrow – if he found out how much we have eaten we would not get any eggs on Sunday," said George. Their father was away for a few nights carrying out maintenance work on a large boat on another part of the canal. As they neared the house they heard the sound of their mother crying loudly.

"Mina mou, Mina mou..." (My Minas, my Minas.)

The children rushed inside but were held back by well-meaning neighbours. In the kitchen they could see their father lying on the table covered by a wet sheet. His face was black and he was crying out in pain. A doctor stood on one side of him and a priest on the other.

"What has happened to our father?" yelled George.

"Pa, Pa," the girls cried.

"Mama what has happened?" demanded George.

Their mother was not able to speak but she pulled her children into her arms, sobbing loudly.

Two women from the neighbourhood took the children outside to the courtyard.

"They must be told," said one woman.

"Your father has been burnt in a fire on a boat," said Anna, the next-door neighbour.

Minas had been replacing a handrail for the stairs going below deck when an explosion beneath him had blown him off his feet, causing him to fall down the stairs into the fire which was burning out of control. He managed to get to his feet but collapsed as soon as he had struggled back on deck. He and several men had been badly burned and brought ashore to be seen by a company doctor at once. His burns were so extensive he could not survive. The only thing that could be done for him was to give him opium and let him die. The drug helped somewhat but still he died in agony at home surrounded by his wife and four children.

When a father, the only breadwinner, dies, the lives of the whole family change dramatically. Plans for George to stay at school and study to become a teacher or to get a job in a bank were now dashed forever. The girls had also been destined to stay at school longer and who knows how their lives could have turned out.

The company paid the widow a small amount but it would not allow the family to live as they had been accustomed. They might have to move into a cheaper home and Katerina would possibly have to do some kind of work. George was only thirteen but now he would have to leave school and begin work as soon as something was found for him. Their world had been turned upside down.

Katerina never fully recovered from her husband's death because they had been together since they were in their early teens. She cried for him every day, asking God for an answer which naturally she never received. She was well loved in the community and was offered a position as housekeeper but declined the offer because she could not leave the safety of her home. Instead she did washing, ironing, mending and needlework at home with the help of her daughters. Fortunately George had learnt some carpentry from his father and was able to begin work as an apprentice almost at once. Nevertheless the family situation had suddenly changed from their being comfortable to being poor.

George took his responsibility as head of the family very seriously and worked hard, always thinking of everyone else before himself. Dora, who had always been close to her mother, remained at home to look after her and help with the work. Katerina became more reclusive and never went further than the front door. The two younger girls were both happily married before their eighteenth birthdays which took a big load off George's shoulders, but still he cared for his mother as she was emotionally fragile.

Around 1925 George was requested by the company to travel to Port Said to work for six weeks on an important project. He found accommodation in a pension near the canal and was able to walk to work each day. As he walked daily a young woman who lived near his pension also walked along the same streets to the local school where she worked as a teacher. On the third day they began to speak to each other and by the end of the first week George was in love. Her name was Amalia and he was smitten by her beauty and intelligence. When he told her about his family and how he had to take responsibility for them from such a young age she loved him for his mature, caring attitude. He was introduced to Amalia's family by the owner of the pension and made a good impression on them. In the evening the couple sat at a local cafe with friends and got to know each other well. After spending as much time together as they were able it was soon time for George to return to Ismailia. He realised he had to make a quick decision so as they walked home one evening he stopped Amalia and waited for the others who continued walking to be out of earshot.

"Amalia, I know we have not known each other very long but as I have to return to Ismalia I cannot go without telling you that I love you and want you to be my wife."

Amalia smiled up at him and raised her hand to caress his cheek.

"I was hoping you would ask me. I love you George and I don't know what I would do without you now," she answered, moving into his arms and lowering the parasol she was carrying to hide behind. Prior to that day they had only kissed on the cheek but now that they were to be married they kissed passionately and wondered how they had waited so long.

They became engaged before he left and planned to marry after Easter in Ismailia because George's mother, Katerina, would not travel to Port Said even for her son's wedding. When George went home to tell his mother the good news she was thrilled for him and began making plans. Sadly, during the Easter celebrations Katerina became unwell. She complained of abdominal pain which came and went over several days. She refused to see a doctor thinking she would recover and stayed in bed, eating nothing and drinking very little.

"Ma, we can afford a doctor," said George.

"I don't need a doctor, just let me stay in bed and rest. I will drink camomile tea, that will help."

After three days the pain stopped and she declared she was well again.

"See, I told you I would be better with rest and camomile tea."

Unfortunately she was not better and overnight she developed a high fever and more pain. George insisted on calling the doctor but it was too late. Her appendix had burst and she died several days later of peritonitis. The family was devastated to lose their mother in such a dreadful way. It seemed to Dora that their lives were always being punctuated by tragedy and she began to go to church daily asking the priest for answers to their sad life. He could only answer "Etan thelima Theou." (It's God's will.")

24

George and Amalia in Ismailia

The wedding between George and Amalia had to be postponed because of the bereavement. They wrote to each other weekly and George went once to Port Said to visit Amalia. Once the mourning period was over they decided to marry in Port Said where Amalia's parents and family lived because Amalia was going to be living in Ismailia. They had a lovely wedding in the large Greek Orthodox church with George's niece and nephew holding the candles at the altar. Amalia's parents were quite well off and put on a wonderful party for the couple in the town square near where they lived. The tables set outside in the warm evening air were laden with delicious food and wine. A group of musicians played and sang long into the night and everyone danced and sang along with the familiar songs.

George and Amalia danced with the other guests and as evening became night they danced in each other's arms, both aware of the closeness of the other and their need to become intimate. George drew her closer and whispered in her ear, "Amalia, there have been so many obstacles that have prevented us from marrying and being alone for so long; why are we waiting now?"

Amalia drew her head back to smile at him. "Let's go then."

George and Amalia slipped away to be alone at last. Their first night together was a wonderful beginning to a very happy life together.

George continued to work for the Suez Canal Company and Amalia joined Dora in the family home and helped to run the household. The two women got on well together and Dora was a great help when Amalia was pregnant or tending a new baby. By 1931 Amalia had given birth to three daughters and they were a very contented family. The children — Katerina, Maria and Joanna — were all intelligent healthy siblings who were taught to read and write at a young age by Amalia who was determined to see her children all educated to the same level as she had been.

George's sister Dora continued to live with them and was a great help with the day-to-day running of the home when the children were little. She was a particularly good cook as her mother had taught her all the Kasiot recipes. Her specialities were stuffed vegetables, dolmathes, moussaka, tiropita and fava, all things the family loved to eat. The little girls would ask for their favourites and help Dora to make them. She loved to cook for the family and even did some cooking for special events in the village. A family friend who owned a restaurant asked for her help when his wife became too sick to work. What started out as a temporary arrangement became an ongoing job for Dora. She eventually took over as head cook and trained several young up-and-coming cooks. The running of the restaurant was left to her as her employer also became ill and died following his wife's death. The owner's daughter approached Dora asking if she would like to buy the restaurant as she herself was not interested in keeping it. She had seen her parents work themselves into the grave and would not contemplate doing the same. Dora was shocked at the offer and did not think it would be possible until she talked to George and Amalia. They discussed the proposition over a few days and decided that they would buy the restaurant between the three of them.

When they took over Dora was still the main cook and was in control of the kitchen. George, who could cook a little, was on a steep learning curve to increase his knowledge and ability. Every night after the customers had gone he would hang fresh yogurt in muslin to drain off the whey so he could make tzatziki each morning when he returned from the market. Amalia was in charge of producing the delicious syrup-soaked Greek sweets. Each day she would make either baklava or galaktoboureko. It was hard work but they enjoyed working together and the children, who were all in secondary school now, could walk home together or walk to the restaurant at the end of the school day.

The girls were very different. The eldest, Katerina, was tall, light-skinned and beautiful. She had the longest legs and the prettiest smile of any girl at school. Maria and Joanna were not as tall or as beautiful as their older sister and although they loved her, one of them, Maria, was envious of Katerina's good looks. Katerina confided in Maria that she was in love with a young man she had met at the market. Sometimes she went to the market with her father and on one occasion she and Harry had made eyes at each other. After that day she went with her father as often as possible hoping to see Harry. Eventually they began to seek each other out and meet secretly. Harry was charming and handsome but not educated or well off or ever likely to be. During their secret meetings their kisses became more and more ardent and both longed for more intimacy.

"Will you marry me, Katerina?" Harry whispered into Katerina's ear as he held her against him.

"Oh yes, yes, I would love to marry you, but I don't think my family will allow me to marry yet."

"We could run away together and when we return they will make us marry," Harry replied.

So they made a plan to leave one night when her parents were busy in the restaurant. Katerina was so excited but also worried that her parents would think that something sinister had happened to her if she just disappeared. It was for this reason that she confided again in her sister Maria and told her of the plan to run away with Harry.

"Maria, please promise not to tell my secret until morning, I am only telling you so that you can tell our parents tomorrow and they will know that I am okay."

Maria promised but she was jealous of her sister and very angry, so as soon as her sister left she had second thoughts. The sisters had been brought up to be chaste and to keep themselves for their wedding night. Maria assumed that Katerina was going to lose her virginity and she was concerned. She ran to the restaurant and raised the alarm. Her parents were enraged and were easily able to identify who Harry was and they rushed to his family home. They were too late, the couple had already left and were headed out of the town via the smaller side streets. Harry had arranged to take Katerina to the home of a friend who had asked no questions. Katerina was very nervous and although they had the house to themselves they did not make love. The romantic feelings Katerina felt for Harry were overshadowed by her fear of what an impulsive thing she had done. Harry did not force her but he was disappointed that their plan had not gone as he wanted.

"Harry, I am sorry but I think I have made a mistake, not about you but what I have done to my parents," she said. Really she was thinking she had made a mistake about the whole thing and she really didn't want to get married at all. Well, not yet anyway.

"It's all right Katerina, I understand, but will your parents force us to marry or will they force us apart?"

"I don't know what they will do. I'll tell them everything and we shall see."

Harry walked with Katerina to her home, where she stopped him at the door and asked him to wait outside.

"I'll go inside and see them first."

"I think I should come in with you."

"No."

When Katerina walked into the house her parents just stared at her. Then her father said, "Well where is your husband."

"He is not my husband."

"Oh yes he is," he replied.

"But nothing happened between us."

"I don't care, he is your husband – or he will be soon."

"But I am not sure if I really want to get married."

"Well you should have thought about that before you did such a dreadful thing."

"What do you mean? Pa, I'm sorry, I made a mistake."

"Bring him inside."

They were married as soon as it could be arranged and they did not live happily ever after. Katerina's schooling ended abruptly, she moved into a small house with Harry's parents and began work with Harry and by the time she was twenty she had two baby boys, Yanni and George. Harry adored Katerina and although she loved him she knew she should have waited and at least finished her schooling. Anyway it was too late now but she had her two beautiful boys and a husband who loved her. Amalia was a devoted grandmother and made sure the boys had clothing and plenty of children's books, hoping to start their interest in reading. She also visited her daughter as often as possible, more often than her husband George knew.

The second daughter, Maria, met and married Kosta and her parents, who were more than happy with this union, put on a wonderful wedding and reception for them at their restaurant. Kosta worked in a French bank which was a much respected job and his parents were well known and liked in the community, so everyone was happy.

After several years the youngest daughter Joanna disappointed her parents even more than Katerina had by falling in love with a young Egyptian man who was a Muslim. Had he been of the Coptic religion they would have accepted him but as they were Greek Orthodox they would not give permission to Joanna to marry Ahmed. Joanna was headstrong and took her initiative from her sister and eloped with Ahmed. Unlike her sister, she did not come back home repentant but stayed away for weeks and only returned after she was married. Her father was so angry with her that he would not let her inside the house. Amalia cried and blamed herself for her two daughters' bad behaviour.

"We left them alone too often; I should have been home all the time," she wailed. "We have made money in the restaurant but we have paid dearly." Amalia became depressed and looked to her eldest daughter for comfort and company.

After a visit to see Katerina she said to George, "I am unhappy and I think Katerina is unhappy and she has more than paid for her mistake. She has named her second son after you and I think it's time we put it all behind us."

"What are you suggesting?"

"Can we bring them to live with us now? Harry can join us in the business, he is hard-working and has more than proved himself as a good husband and father. Also I am feeling very tired lately and it would help me enormously."

George thought about Amalia's idea for a week or more and then went to see Harry with the offer, which was very gratefully accepted.

Katerina was so happy to return to her family home and now that her sisters were married there was plenty of room for them all. Amalia taught Harry to make the sweets and she spent more time at home with her daughter and grandsons. The little boys loved their yiayia (grandmother) and brought their books to her to read to them as often as possible and asked her to sing and play games with them.

Although Amalia felt better now that she was away from the restaurant she was shocked but delighted when she realised that she was pregnant. Being in her late forties she had not imagined she would have another baby, especially not now. When she told George he grabbed her and spun her around laughing out loud.

"That's wonderful! I am so happy, what a wonderful surprise, we are so clever."

A baby boy, Minas, was born and Amalia's happiness soared as she looked at the little button nose and rosebud mouth in his sweet little squashed newborn face. She was so in love with her dark-haired baby boy she thought she might burst with joy. George was thrilled to have a boy to name after his father at last and happy to see his wife so happy and with a baby at her breast again.

25

Political unrest, Suez Crisis, 1956

The restaurant was a big success and became a place where many important business lunches were held by local politicians, bankers and company directors. George was aware of the subjects being discussed and was alerted to problems between the governments of France, England and Egypt with the Suez Canal Company. One of his clients warned him of political unrest and possibly worse and advised him to get his money out of Egypt. George spoke to the family about the things he heard and with the assistance of Kosta he transferred as much money as he was able into an Athenian bank.

Although the Suez Canal had been built by the French and Egyptians, a large proportion of the company shares were sold to the English in 1875 so this meant the company was mainly owned by the English and French.

In the early 1950s the Egyptian people, ruled by President Gamal Abdel Nasser, were not happy with this state of affairs. The French and particularly the English had a strong hold in Egypt but they wanted more control of the Suez Canal. In 1956 the Suez Crisis occurred – also called the Tripartite Aggression – in which Egypt was attacked by Israel, France and England. The aim was to regain Western control of the canal and remove President Nasser. The Egyptians fought back but were defeated. However they managed to block the canal and no ships could use it. The United Nations, USA and the Soviet Union forced the three invaders to withdraw causing humiliation to the English and strengthening Nasser's position.

With the canal closed many jobs no longer existed and the future became uncertain. Everything changed: people left in droves, businesses failed, shops and schools began to close. Life as they had known it was over. George and Amalia felt as if they were stuck; they could not sell their house or their restaurant. The restaurant did not make money any more and there were houses for sale all over the city. They were worried about their property but their safety and future security were more important. They closed the restaurant and decided to go to Greece.

George's older sister Dora refused to leave. It broke her heart to leave the business they had worked so hard to establish and it broke her heart to leave Ismailia. She was adamant that she would not leave Egypt no matter what. No one could change her mind. She wanted to stay in the house alone. She closed off the upper floor of the house and lived downstairs on her own.

The day before the family left for Greece they went to see Joanna and Ahmed. This was the first time they had met Joanna and Ahmed's children, their grandchildren, and they had to say goodbye in the same hour. George, Amalia and Dora between them decided to give Joanna the deeds to the restaurant building which had been transferred into her name.

George and Amalia Mavrikakis along with their other two daughters, their husbands, their grandchildren and their new baby boy Minas all left Ismailia and Egypt and travelled to Athens to start a new life.

26

Return to Greece

The Mavrikakis family settled in Pireaus, the port of Athens. They decided to open a taverna which was more casual than a restaurant, and as it was by the sea it would specialise in fresh seafood. They bought a struggling business along the seafront and set about renovating the building in the hope of increasing the clientele and making the business a success. The shop was painted white and trimmed with light blue, the navy blue rush-bottomed chairs were given a new coat of paint and the tablecloths were blue and white check. Fishing paraphernalia decorated the walls and ceilings giving it the appearance of an inviting island taverna which they named Poseidon after the Greek god of the sea.

To help launch Poseidon one Sunday they had a free night for some of the locals. They employed three musicians and a singer to entertain the crowd so everyone could dance and sing. It was a wonderful night and helped to introduce the business. Because it was near the port where boats left for the nearby island of Salamina it became very popular with tourists when they disembarked after a day out.

Kosta and Maria lived in the city near the bank in which Kosta worked and Harry and Katerina lived with George and Amalia. Katerina walked her children to school each morning and helped George and Harry with food preparation during the day. Amalia was happy at home with her adored baby Minas, happier now than at any other time in her life.

Each afternoon Katerina watered the pots of basil that were placed along the front of the tavern. When the hose sprayed the verdant leaves the strong aroma of the herb filled the air.

"What is that herb?" said a male voice from one of the outside tables.

"It is basil," Katerina replied, smiling at the attractive man. She was surprised someone would not know about basil. "Don't you know basil?"

"I was not sure," he answered.

"We use it in our salads and some other dishes." She picked a tiny sprig and passed it to the man to smell and taste.

When the man took the basil from Katerina his eyes held her gaze in a way she had not expected. It was a look that produced such a strong feeling within her that she was shocked. She looked back at this handsome man and knew she was blushing. Averting her eyes she went inside the taverna.

The next day the same man was there again waiting for her to go outside to water the basil.

"What is your name?"

"Katerina."

"I am Michael."

"Are you on holiday?" asked Katerina.

"Yes. I live in America and I am here trying to improve my Greek, that's why I like talking to you."

"I am happy to help. I am usually here when my children are at school."

The following day when Katerina took the children to school he was waiting for her and they walked to the taverna together speaking a mixture of Greek and English. After that he caught up with her every day as she walked to or from the school but never again at the taverna. Katerina knew he was not only interested in speaking Greek with her after he confessed that he really had known about the herb basil.

As they walked along he touched her hand or her arm and she felt a frisson which made her want a little more. She knew she was playing with fire and that Harry would not be happy about this friendship. She found Michael charming and flattering but she was shocked when he asked her to go with him to his hotel room.

"No I can't do that, I am a married woman."

"No one will know, we will be careful."

"But if I am found out I will lose everything."

"Will you at least think about it?"

"I will think about it, but I don't think I can."

Katerina thought of nothing else over the next day and she could not make up her mind. The more she thought about Michael the more aroused she became and the thought of being in bed with him drove her crazy. She did not sleep that night, she tossed and turned and had to get up and get away from Harry because she felt guilty. At daybreak she had decided that she would go with Michael to his hotel room.

Katerina showered and put on pretty underwear. Her heart beat fast and she could not eat breakfast. Harry left the house before she and the children began their walk to school. When they finally left the house she was dizzy with excitement and apprehension. At the school she waved goodbye to the children and looked around for Michael but could not see him so she began her walk towards the taverna as usual.

Katerina took her time, expecting to see Michael at any moment but he did not appear. When she arrived at the corner of the street she saw Harry rush towards the taverna and hurry inside. She spent a regular day at the taverna doing the usual chores then left a little earlier than normal to meet the children. Disappointed but also a little relieved that Michael was not to be seen, she arrived at the school and waited for the children to come out so they could walk home together.

Michael did not show up the next day or the next. On the third day two policemen arrived at the taverna to speak to them about a murdered man called Michael Savas who had been found strangled in his hotel room.

"We have been told the man was seen here and that you Kyria [Mrs] have been seen walking with him in the local streets," said one of the policemen.

Harry looked startled when he heard this and glared at Katerina.

"He was found by his wife who has just arrived in Greece," the policeman added.

Katerina was shocked because he had told her he was not married; she said nothing.

"Why was he with you, Kyria; is he related to you?"

"No," said Katerina, "he asked me to help him speak Greek."

"When did you last see him?" asked the policeman.

"Three days ago I think."

"Why did he walk with you?"

"I told him I had to work while my children were at school, that was the only spare time I had."

"Was there anything else between you?"

"No, no, not at all."

The policemen spoke briefly with Harry and George then they thanked them and left.

Harry was so angry with Katerina he began to shake.

"How could you do such a thing, people will talk about you, you will lose your good reputation."

"I did nothing wrong. Maybe I was silly but I did nothing wrong."

Katerina remembered seeing Harry that day hurrying into the tavern and she felt sick with guilt.

'This is all my fault, my vanity has caused me to almost betray my husband and now he has killed a man,' she thought. She sobbed all day as she went about her chores. When she and Harry were alone at last she asked him, "Did you kill that man Harry?"

Harry turned to her with the angriest look on his face.

"NO I DID NOT, I WOULD NEVER KILL ANYONE!"

"But I saw you rush into the taverna just ahead of me, what were you doing?"

"I WAS OUT LOOKING FOR YOU!"

"Harry, I am sorry but I just had to ask you."

"You really do not know me and I certainly don't know you," he said.

Several days later the police returned and Harry was arrested and charged with murder. He was taken to the police lockup and held in detention. Harry, who was a law-abiding man, was shocked and ashamed to find himself locked up by the police. He was not allowed to have visitors. He lost his appetite and could not sleep.

Several of the hotel staff had described a man they had seen sneaking into the hotel on the morning of the murder. In the minds of the police their descriptions fitted Harry accurately. After some days the witnesses were finally taken to the lockup to identify Harry but when they saw him they were adamant it was not the same man. One of the witnesses actually knew Harry, and also George swore that Harry was with him in the restaurant at the time of the murder, so the charges were dropped.

Harry had spent almost a week in the lockup and although he was cleared of the murder, it had a depressing effect on him. His relationship with Katerina disintegrated. The couple barely spoke – in fact Harry did not want to speak to anyone, and became too despondent to return to work. He spent his days out in a boat fishing or just sitting at the port looking out to sea. He did not eat much and began to lose weight. He looked awful. He would not sleep in bed with Katerina, preferring to sleep on a divan.

Katerina begged him to talk to her but he would not respond. She could not reach him no matter how hard she tried. George had to employ a man to take his place in the taverna hoping that it would be temporary but after several months Harry was no better.

Harry was devastated by what had happened to him because he was basically a good man and he had been wronged on two counts. He was grateful the charge against him had been dropped but he felt people were talking about him behind his back. He could not look at Katerina, let alone talk to her.

One day Harry went out in his boat but he never returned. His boat drifted in on the tide containing only his fishing gear and his shoes.

George wrote to his sister Dora who had insisted on staying in Egypt and begged her to come to Greece to help them. Surprisingly she agreed and turned up less than a month after Harry went missing. The house in Ismailia was vacant but still for sale. Dora had become quite lonely after the family left because more and more of the people she had known for so long had also left Egypt.

Having Dora with them helped enormously as she was a no-nonsense, hard-working woman who immediately took over the work Harry had been doing. Amalia now walked with Katerina to school each day and they both worked in the taverna, thus sharing the physical and emotional burden between them all.

Katerina was never tempted again to even look at another man and longed for Harry who she now realised had been the best husband she could have wished for.

**

Michael the Womaniser

Oh what a beauty and so innocent. She is like a ripe peach waiting to be plucked. Yes she is married and has children but her husband is obviously just a simple peasant. She will be easy to snare to add to the number of women I have had.
Fortunately my fat, ugly, nagging wife will not be around for a few weeks so I am free to do what I like. A couple of days should be enough to rope her in and then in no time into my bed. Women are so easy to fool.

**

27

A stranger appears, 1970

Tourism in Greece had always existed but in the 1970s it began to boom. Athens was the first place people thought of when travelling to Greece. New hotels were built and tavernas and restaurants opened. Everything was inexpensive and tourists arrived not only from America but from faraway places such as Australia and New Zealand and they had money to spend. It was a successful time for the family and they were able to buy some property and save quite a bit of money. By 1970 the children were running the taverna and their parents were taking a well-earned break except for the busiest times, when everyone helped.

One warm evening a well-dressed stranger appeared at the taverna. None of the children recognised him but he knew the children.

"Where are your parents?" he asked.

"At home," said Minas (now a grown man) "but they will be in later for a bite to eat."

"I will wait here to see them," he said.

George, Amalia and Katerina arrived at the taverna about 10pm. They walked in smiling and happy to see the tables full, music playing and patrons dancing.

"There is a man here waiting to see you," said Minas, pointing to a table where the man was seated on his own.

Katerina was the first one to look at him and her hands flew to her face as she said, "Harry! Harry where have you been all this time? We thought you were dead!"

The three of them rushed to the table so happy to see him and impatient to find out where he had been and what he had been doing.

"I am sorry for going away and telling no-one but I was so unhappy I just needed to be away from you all to find myself again. I thought if I could not recover my peace of mind I would stay away and you would always think me dead. Now I am on top of the world and so I have come back. I hope you can all forgive me and welcome me back."

Everyone talked at once. "Of course we want you back! Where have you been?"

"I found work on one of the large ships leaving the port here at Piraeus. I worked on the ship in the kitchen for several years then I went ashore and to Thessaloniki where I worked as head chef in a big restaurant. I have learned about cooking the French and Italian way and I have saved my money. I would like Katerina to be my wife again." He looked at Katerina as he said this and she smiled at him. "I want that also," she said.

Harry was patient and courted Katerina as if they were engaged to be married. He took her out for dinner or for long walks and then away for a weekend so they became husband and wife again. For both of them it was like having a new lover and they were extremely happy and in love.

"Was the killer ever found?" asked Harry.

"Yes, his brother-in-law killed him; apparently it was because he was always chasing other women and he had brought great shame on his wife's family."

Harry returned to the tavern and took over the cooking which now became a bit more sophisticated and the menu more varied and exciting as they introduced other European cuisines. George had turned seventy and he and Amalia began to feel superfluous in the taverna and left most of the work to the others. Now having plenty of spare time George suggested that they go away for a holiday to one of the Greek islands. They decided to visit Kasos.

28

Return to Kasos, late 1970s

It had been almost seventy years since George had left Kasos as a baby and he felt quite excited at the thought of seeing his island again. They went by ferry and arrived early on a beautiful sunny morning. Their first impression was that it seemed very quiet, very simple and unspoiled. A man at the port carried their bags on the back of a donkey to a nearby hotel where they checked in thinking they would stay for a week or two. After unpacking they set out for a walk to see what there was in the little village of Free. They found a charming little port where fishermen were selling their catch and sorting and repairing nets. Behind the port was a pleasant whitewashed church and beyond that a few shops and a taverna.

People looked at them with curiosity and they were soon engaged in conversation with several of the villagers. When George told them he had been born there seventy years ago he was inundated with questions about who his parents were, what they had done in Egypt and where they had lived lately. People invited them to their homes and they were treated very hospitably.

George knew there was property on the island that belonged to him which he hoped to claim so he set about locating it. He was directed to someone in the council who had papers regarding property ownership.

"Your property is not in Free, it's up the mountainside in Agia Marina," the man said. "I will take you to see it if you like."

There were few cars on the island as the population was small and not very wealthy. There were a few trucks and the ever-faithful donkeys which were hired to take them up a steep winding road to the village of Agia Marina.

"I think we are too heavy for these poor old donkeys," said Amalia as she alighted from the old, worn-out saddle.

"No, that's what they are bred for, they are strong animals."

"Still, I don't like to see such small sweet animals working like this on a hot day."

When they reached their destination they discovered narrow meandering streets containing small white houses and a church, a few paddocks growing vegetables and others with chickens scratching in the dirt. Their house was easy to find but was a bit of a disappointment. It was just a shell – four walls and a roof, the windows and doors boarded over. Weeds grew inside and out of the building and stray cats with kittens hid amidst the wreckage.

"Well, I don't think we can stay here," said George.

"No, but it could be repaired," replied Amalia.

Disenchanted by the house they returned to Free and decided to go for a swim. They were told of a beach about ten minutes' walk further along the coast where it was pleasant to swim. They found the beach easily and, dropping their towels on the sand, they dived into the inviting sea. Floating and swimming in the warm calm water they looked up at the imposing mountains surrounding the bay, the drystone walls and purple thyme bushes, and were enchanted by it all.

Amalia pointed up high and said, "Look at that family with the donkey walking down that steep rocky track."

"Where?" said George.

"There – oh no, they have gone," said Amalia.

"You're seeing things."

"I definitely saw them. I suppose they changed their minds and turned back."

The little beach that fringed the bay was a semi-circle of white sand the shape of a crescent moon, lapped by gentle waves.

"Do you know what this little spot needs?" asked George.

"Yes I know what you are going to say," Amalia replied.

"Well, don't you think a little taverna would be perfect here?"

"Yes I agree."

"People could swim in the morning, have a bite to eat then go back to the beach for a snooze. Then at night they could watch the sun set as they eat and listen to the waves lapping at the shore."

There were a few old disused buildings facing the sea and any one of them could easily be transformed into a suitable tavern.

"I am going to see if we can rent or buy one of these buildings," said George. "If I am successful I will ask Minas to come and help and then he can take over when it's all done."

Some people were very keen to sell their property because to them it was useless as they did not have the money to renovate. George bought one of the buildings and arranged to rent a small house nearby. When they left the island their intention was to return as soon as they were able to arrange a builder and the materials to renovate.

It took them over a year and a lot of help from Minas and George's sister Dora to get the taverna up and running. The front of the building was open and looked on to the crescent-shaped beach so they called it Taverna Feggari (Taverna moon).

Minas took over the running of the business and employed local young men and women to work for him. Therefore Dora, George and Amalia could really take a back seat and enjoy semi-retirement.

George could not sit still for long so he began restoration of the family house in the village of Agia Marina. It was a small house but rustic and full of charm. The roof was replaced, larger windows were fitted and a new kitchen and bathroom were installed. The walls were freshly whitewashed and it looked as good as new so Amalia began to establish a garden. She planted a bougainvillea at the front of the house and roses along the front fence and even adopted two stray cats to keep mice away. Amalia asked George to make window boxes for the front windows where she planted red geraniums. They moved into their new house in early summer but Dora stayed with Minas to keep house for him so he could be close to the taverna.

29

George born, 1980

Minas enjoyed running his own taverna and he relished the company of the friendly, noisy village men. They sat at his tables and drank ouzo and laughed and sang and argued into the night. Many of the older men and some younger would play with their worry beads as they sat and solved the world's problems. He bought fresh fish from some of these men who were fishermen and they gave him the first pick of their catch.

He became very popular with the young single women on the island and his mother urged him to choose one of them for a wife.

"All in good time Ma, all in good time," he teased her.

Several more Kasiot families moved back to the island from Athens and one of these families had a daughter who captured Minas' heart at one glance. Her name was Melina but Minas called her Meli (honey).

"I will call you Meli," said Minas, "because you are as sweet as honey."

"What will I call you?"

"Just call me your husband and I will be happy."

They had a whirlwind romance and a wonderful wedding on an autumn evening in the little church in Free and then a party at Taverna Feggari. Everyone on the island was invited to the festivities and most came. The couple went to Crete for a honeymoon and returned to live in the rented house. Dora tactfully offered to move and George and Amalia invited her to live with them again. Minas offered Dora a donkey to bring her down to the taverna on the days she worked but she refused, saying she would prefer to walk as it would keep her healthy.

Everyone was happy and when the newlyweds announced they were expecting a baby, it seemed life was just so wonderful it could not get any better. But life has its ups and downs and when George's sister Dora suffered a stroke it was a sad time for the whole family. Her condition was severe; she did not regain consciousness and died within a week.

"We have lost one of the dearest people," said Amalia. "She has helped and supported us so much, we will miss her always."

The birth of Minas and Meli's baby helped to ease the pain they all felt. The baby was a boy and of course they named him George. Baby George was adored by his parents and grandparents and he was given a lot of attention, therefore he talked at a young age and had a broad vocabulary by age three. He was a bright, happy boy who made people laugh and charmed everyone who met him. He was able to read and write before he began school and always excelled at his school work.

As he went through school his parents often talked about his obvious intelligence and wondered what he would do when he finished school. Like many parents they wanted him to be a doctor but George had his heart set on being a secondary school teacher. After finishing his schooling on Kasos he went to Athens to live with his aunt and attend university. His intention was to teach at one of the island schools where he knew there was a great need. His first position was in a secondary school in Crete where he taught history, literature and creative writing. He was very keen on writing stories about the history of the Greek islands because he knew they each had their own tales to tell.

George moved into a shared house with other young teachers where he lived during the school term. During the long summer break he went home to Kasos to help his parents in their Taverna Feggari. It was during one of these long term breaks that he met the love of his life, Poppy Mavrikakis.

Part Three

30

George in Australia, 2011

Poppy was nervous and excited as she drove to Melbourne airport to meet George who was flying in from Greece. She was far too early and had to wait for more than an hour outside the big doors of the arrivals hall. During the time she was waiting she thought, 'What if he missed his plane? Or what if he just decided not to come?' Various other irrational thoughts went through her head as she watched the doors open and close.

A steady flow of people emerged through the doors and when she had almost given up hope George walked out and looked around.

"George! George! Over here, I am here," called Poppy, waving madly.

George saw her and a huge smile lit up his face. They hurried over to each other and hugged for ages, not saying anything at all. When they finally did speak Poppy said, "kalosorises [welcome]!"

"You have been learning more Greek, that's wonderful," George replied.

Once they were in Poppy's car and heading towards the freeway they were so excited they both talked at the same time, asking questions but not hearing the answers and finally just laughing at how silly they were.

Eventually they calmed down and Poppy said "I am taking you to my home tonight where you will be staying and tomorrow afternoon I will take you to meet my parents. Unfortunately my brother will not be at home, he is working in Berlin. My parents are expecting us for dinner and then we can stay the night because my father has something to tell us which he says will take a long time. They wanted to come and meet you tonight but I said I wanted to have you all to myself on your first night here."

"That's wise, we have a lot of time to make up and lot of love to catch up on." George smiled at her and reached over to caress her cheek.

George was tired from the long flight in economy class but not too tired to make love to Poppy. They fell into bed and stayed wrapped in each other's arms all night, waking once or twice delighted to see one another and to make love again.

Poppy's house was in a semi-rural village at the bottom of a mountain. In the morning George was woken by the dawn chorus of kookaburras and magpies right outside the window. When he got out of bed he was amazed at the beautiful green hills he could see in the distance and kangaroos in the paddocks nearby. They made love again then took a shower together, admiring each other's youthful beauty.

"I had forgotten just how delicious you are Poppy," said George.

Poppy smiled at him and turned off the water. "We will never get any-where today if we don't get out of the shower and put some clothes on."

31

Poppy's parents

In the afternoon Poppy drove George to her parents' home to meet them for the first time.

"I am a bit nervous to meet them," said George.

"Don't be nervous, my parents are wonderful open-minded people and they are longing to meet you, and Mum will be cooking up a storm for you."

"What is cooking up a storm?"

Poppy laughed, "It means she will cook all her best dishes and lots of food and there will be leftovers for the next week!"

Poppy's mother Beth did cook up a storm and when the happy couple walked in and saw the spread they looked at each other and laughed.

"What's so funny?" said Beth.

"Just all the food," Poppy replied. "Where is Dad?"

"I am here," called Poppy's father Christos as he came inside.

Christos went straight to George and shook his hand, "Welcome George, Beth and I are so happy that you are here at last."

Beth gave George a kiss on both cheeks and invited him to sit down.

The meal was delicious and the conversation was easy and friendly. Christos and Beth were taken by George's good humour and friendly personality. Poppy went to the kitchen with her mother who said to her, "Not only is he handsome but also a lovely young man. I can see why you have fallen in love with him."

"Oh Mum, I'm so glad you feel that way because he is definitely the man I want to spend the rest of my life with."

George had noticed some paintings that hung in the hall and the living room and asked, "Who painted the pictures of Greece?"

"They were all done by my father Minas, come and see and I will tell you about them."

They spent some time viewing all the paintings then Christos took George into the study where a large canvas which was divided into three panels hung on the wall.

"This is a picture my father painted. He did it to help him cope with the cruelty of the war and some of the things he experienced that he would never discuss with us."

George looked at the painting for quite a long time.

"There is certainly a story in this painting and it is full of pathos," George said.

"After I have told you the family history you can have another look at it," Christos answered.

After the meal they sat drinking coffee, when Poppy said to George, "There are some things Dad has found out about the coincidences of our names."

"Yes," said Christos, "Between my father and one of my uncles who was given some family history some years ago and by asking all the older members of the family, we have compiled quite a good manuscript."

"Can you tell us now Dad?"

"Okay, but if we start now we will be up all night," said Christos as he placed on the table a large folder of papers and a few photographs.

"As I told Poppy, it is a sad story and goes back to the island of Kasos where there was a massacre by the Turks in 1824."

32

Kasos 1824 and beyond, as told by Poppy's father

Christos was only a toddler when his parents Minas and Maria left the island of Kasos following the massacre in 1824. Along with his brother George and his two cousins Eleni and Kalliopi they resettled in Sitia on the island of Crete in a little house with only two rooms. Minas fished and Maria slowly established a small herd of goats and eventually began cheese making. The children soon settled into the village and made friends with other children. George and Christos were very protective of their cousins, they were brought up as brothers and sisters and all attended the village school and helped their parents after school.

The family thrived on hard work and determination which enabled them eventually to buy a slightly bigger house with a small enclosed garden. When Christos was in his early teens his brother George left Crete and returned to Kasos. Christos was resentful towards George for leaving. He thought his brother very selfish and vowed he would never leave his parents because of what they had been through. Although there was one less mouth to feed, there was also now one less person to contribute to the upkeep and income of the household. Christos was forced to take on more fishing and more gardening to help his father. Eleni and Kalliopi became competent cheese makers and went with Maria to the market twice a week to sell their produce.

Both girls were very pretty and always caused heads to turn in admiration as they walked alongside Maria. Several young men actually approached Minas and asked to court the girls but although he wanted the girls to marry one day, he was in no hurry to see them gone. However Eleni was wooed by one of her admirers and eventually married him and moved into the little two-roomed house the family had first lived in. Kalliopi was younger and showed no interest in the admiring men, preferring to stay at home and help Maria.

George came from Kasos to visit the family who tried to persuade him to stay but he insisted it was just a visit and returned to his island after a week. Minas and Maria were sad to see him go again but Kalliopi, who was obviously upset by his departure, seemed quite changed. Maria suspected that she missed George a lot more than before his visit.

During the next year Christos married a lovely girl named Vera who he had known since school. Both sets of parents were delighted with the union as they were all friends and lived close by. The newlyweds moved in with Vera's parents which meant that now Minas and Maria had only Kalliopi with them.

Once again the two young men asked Minas if they could court Kalliopi but as she was not interested, Minas said no to both of them. One of the young men, Manoli, was very persistent and said he would wait, hoping Kalliopi would change her mind.

Two years after his first visit George came again to Crete to see his family and was surprised to find his brother Christos married and Eleni now the mother of two children. His great wish when he returned to Crete was that he could marry his cousin Kalliopi. When they saw each other again they knew they wanted to be together so they approached Minas and Maria who advised them to speak to the priest. The priest would not marry them because they were first cousins and he could not be persuaded otherwise. George refused to accept the decision and he decided to take Kalliopi and elope to Kasos. Kalliopi was quite happy to run off with George and after a few secretive days stashing her belongings in the boat they escaped early one morning.

Kalliopi left a letter for Minas and Maria saying that she had gone with George and if she did not marry him she would die of a broken heart. She added that she would return to see them sometime in the future.

Minas and Maria discovered the letter early in the morning and, hoping they could catch them at the port, they called for Christos and rushed to the port. George's boat had gone and a large crowd was gathered around the dead body of Manoli. The three of them were so shocked they could barely speak. Without becoming involved in conversation with the villagers they went home to speak privately.

"Do not assume that they had anything to do with his death," said Minas. "I know George would not kill anyone deliberately."

"No," agreed Christos, "Not deliberately."

Maria threw her apron over her face and sobbed.

Questions were asked by the authorities but as no witnesses came forward no one was ever named as responsible and it was called an accidental death.

However there was one witness, but he never came forward to speak about what he had seen — the witness was Christos. He had suspected the couple were up to something and had watched them take Kalliopi's possessions to the boat in secret. On the morning they departed he saw them reach the port followed by Manoli but he could not hear what was said. He saw Manoli push George and saw George grab at Manoli who fell and hit his head, then he watched as the couple pushed the boat out and fled. Christos went home without checking on Manoli — it did not occur to him that the unfortunate man was fatally wounded. When Minas and Maria called for him on that morning he did not say anything as they rushed to the port, knowing George's boat would be gone. Afterwards he felt guilty because he had not gone to Manoli's aid and had not said anything about what he had seen. It worried him that people would think him insensitive and he therefore felt even more resentment towards George; after all it was his actions which had caused the problem.

After that Christos rarely spoke his brother's name and was glad that he never visited them again but he knew his mother ached to see the couple. Although Kalliopi was not her own daughter Maria had reared her from birth and breastfed her for almost two years and they had been very close. Maria had no more children after the time they spent up in the mountain when their island was attacked so always thought of Kalliopi as her last baby and she loved her like her own.

33

Minas marries Aspasia, Christos marries Lydia then Anthea, Crete 1870 onwards. Minas born 1920.

Christos and Vera Mavrikakis and their family of two boys and a girl remained on Crete and had a better life than his brother George and Kalliopi on Kasos. His boys Minas and Stavros and daughter Maria all married and had large families. By the time Christos's parents (Minas and Maria) died there were a dozen grandchildren but they never saw those on Kasos.

Around 1870 Christos's son Minas married a girl called Aspasia who lived near Palea Roumata, a mountain village at the western end of Crete. After the wedding he went to live and work with Aspasia's family on their large farm where they grew olives for the table but mainly for making oil. Minas enjoyed the olive harvesting and pressing because it was something he had never done before. They also owned a large herd of goats which ran free in the mountains. Some of the goats were sold for their meat and Aspasia's mother kept a large number of nanny goats for their milk as they were also the local cheese producers. This was something Minas knew about and he was a great asset to his new family as they had no sons, only daughters.

Aspasia's mother was an artistic woman and a nature lover who had not only taught her girls how to make cheese but also instilled in them a love of nature and drawing. In the countryside of Crete there were beautiful wildflowers everywhere which Aspasia encouraged her daughters to draw and to pick and dry to make artistic arrangements to decorate the house. Aspasia could draw very well and her father bought pencils and later water colours so that she could paint. Her favourite subjects were wildflowers and the butterflies that fluttered everywhere in spring and summer. Her paintings were hung in the house and in the shop where they stored and sold their oil and cheese. Customers liked the paintings and sometimes bought them for their own homes. Later, she painted couples in their wedding attire, the women wearing colourful Cretan dresses and the handsome Cretan men in their traditional costumes showing the knee-length boots and baggy pants they wore. They were tall, strong, brave-looking men with large moustaches and often carried daggers at their sides. They were very protective of their families, their land and their island of Crete.

When Minas and Aspasia's children were little she encouraged them to love nature and to draw what they saw when she took them out on nature study excursions as her mother had done. The oldest boy, Christos, was particularly talented and from a young age showed signs of exceeding his mother's artistic ability. He became a portrait painter of great note and his work became well known first in Hania and later all over Crete. Many families were happy to pay for a portrait of the family or the matriarch and patriarch at the time. Only thirty years old in 1900, Christos was sometimes asked to travel further afield to paint important people — or people who wanted to appear important. He travelled to Rethimno to paint the portrait of Mr Petrakis who was a wine merchant. His daughter Lydia saw Christos and asked to be included in the portrait and the father, who could not refuse his daughter anything, agreed. Lydia just wanted to be in a position to make eyes at Christos and win his heart. She did win his heart; Christos fell in love with Lydia and asked her father for her hand in marriage.

They married and were happy for a few years but Lydia had no children and became restless and wanted to return to Rethimno to her adoring father and a more exciting lifestyle. Christos agreed but only if he had a commission to paint a portrait there. Lydia was happy with this arrangement until she had her first baby which changed everything. From then on she wanted only to be with her baby girl. Lydia was a woman who had been seeking something all her young life and when she became a mother she knew motherhood was what she had been looking for. Lydia and Christos adored their little girl Passy (short for Aspasia) and because she was an only child they taught her everything they could. Passy had her father's artistic talent and followed the tradition set by her grandmother of nature walks and painting and drawing. Lydia longed for another baby but none came for another ten years, when they had almost given up hope. Towards the end of an uneventful pregnancy Lydia became very unwell and after a long labour a normal baby was born but Lydia died from blood loss and infection within days of the birth. The family was devastated. A wet nurse was hired to live in and feed the baby and the older girl was cared for by her yiayia (Aspasia).

Christos was very unhappy and at first felt that he could not live without Lydia, but he continued to work and to paint which helped him cope with his grief. When he was nearly fifty years old he decided to take a trip to view the archaeological excavations in Knossos near Heraklion. He had heard about a British archaeologist, Sir Arthur Evans, who had recommenced excavation of the area in 1900. The diggings had been partly excavated in 1878 and had revealed significant historical artefacts.

At the site Christos met Harry Nikakis, another man who was fascinated by the excavation and what was being dug up from the Classical and Hellenic eras. The two became good friends and Harry invited Christos to his home and, because they were travelling to the diggings most days, he asked him to stay with his family so they could travel each day together. While staying at Harry's villa Christos met and fell in love with Harry's daughter, thirty-year-old Anthea. The family had given up hope of her marrying and were thrilled that at last she was to be a bride. The couple were married and travelled back to Christos's home to live. Anthea was a kind woman and was very happy to become stepmother to Christos's two girls. Anthea's love of the garden was her passion and she established a beautiful garden at the family home. Roses were her specialty and Christos loved to paint his beautiful wife in her garden pruning the roses or holding a bloom to her nose as she inhaled the luscious scent.

In 1920 a baby boy was born to Christos and Anthea and he was named Minas. Christos was pleased to have a son to carry on the family name and whom he hoped he could teach to paint. With his mother's love of the garden and his father's ability to paint Minas did become an artist of flowers and people in landscapes. He had seen copies of French impressionist paintings and these inspired him to paint the Cretan countryside with peasants working in the fields or resting in the shade of olive trees. His paintings were exhibited in a studio in Hania and many were bought by the tourists who loved to travel to Greece. Some paintings he reproduced time and time again because they were popular pictures which sold quickly but that did not satisfy him; he preferred to paint a new subject each time.

As an adolescent Minas continued to work in the family business of cheese making and olive growing but his spare time was spent painting in the hills and local countryside. He painted men harvesting the olives and working the huge press that produced the beautiful green-gold oil. He painted young boys herding goats down to be milked and he painted women making cheese in the cheesery. There was a painting of his sisters dressed in white sitting on a blanket in the shade of a fig tree eating the delicious fruit as they laughed together on a warm summer day; another of his parents sitting reading together on a green bench under a huge magnolia tree, the sun sparkling through the large leaves. Most of these pictures were hung in the family home and depicted the idyllic life they lived until the late 1930s.

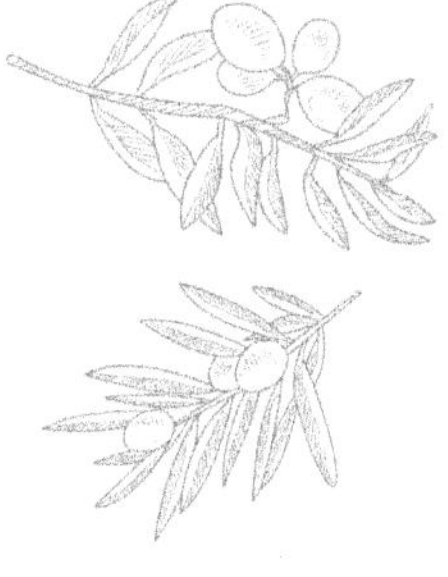

34

WW2, Crete, 1940s

The Second World War broke out in 1939 and in 1941 German and Italian soldiers overran Greece and forced the Allied soldiers on mainland Greece to retreat to Crete. The Allied soldiers were from Greece, Britain, New Zealand and Australia. Hitler wanted to use Crete as a base to launch further attacks in the Mediterranean and beyond so it was important that Germany occupy Crete. The first invasion of Crete was repelled easily by the Allied forces but they misjudged the Germans, who came back with a vengeance. For the first time Germany waged a heavy invasion with paratroopers and gliders. Eyewitnesses said they saw small doll-like figures fall from the sky suspended under silky umbrellas which aided in floating them delicately to the ground. Some of the paratroopers were sitting ducks as they fell visibly to the ground, to be slaughtered savagely before they could disentangle themselves from their parachutes.

The paratrooper invasion continued for ten days and eventually the numbers were enormous. Grisly fights took place between the German invaders and the Allies and awful hand to hand clashes were fought. In many cases the Cretans were not well armed and used whatever they could to fight the invaders. Hundreds of people from both sides were killed. The Cretan men, already known for their courage, were determined to fight and not surrender under any circumstances. Women also took up arms against the invaders.

It became an unwinnable contest and from 29 May 1941, 10,000 Allied soldiers were evacuated from Crete. Those who were unable to leave the island were eventually given the choice of surrendering or escaping into the mountains. Some choose surrender but many fled into the mountains. Later in the year more Allies escaped from the island; only a few remained. The Germans stayed on the island until the end of the war and the civilians and remaining soldiers continued their battle against them.

It was during this time that Minas was caught up in the Resistance. Although he was an artist he still worked on the land so he was strong and healthy. He never questioned his duty as a Cretan man to help defend his island against the hated Germans. As in every war there are some who would rather not be there but had no choice. One morning Minas found two very young German soldiers hiding in one of the outhouses. They were just boys really, of similar age to the young boys tending their goat herd. The young Germans, who looked like brothers, were terrified of him and got down on bended knees crossing themselves and begging not to be killed. Minas was a kind man but these boys, although young, were the enemy and he knew that most Cretans would kill them without thinking. But he could not. He did not know what to do with them so he locked them in the outhouse and went away to think and decide.

He did not sleep that night. He thought he would give them water and bread and turn them out in the morning but then they would surely be killed so he might as well just kill them himself. He tossed and turned, not really able to decide anything so when he rose in the morning he had made a decision but was feeling dreadful. He drank two cups of thick sweet Greek coffee and was just about to approach the outhouse when a neighbour banged on the door shouting.

"Minas, Minas ella, ella [come, come], we have found two German soldiers hiding in your outhouse."

Minas felt his pulse begin to race but said nothing.

"They were seen entering the building by my young son, he told me about them this morning."

Minas held his breath waiting for the next bit of information.

"You don't have to worry though, I have killed them both."

Minas went with his neighbour and was shocked at the sight of the two boys who had certainly been killed in a most violent way. He walked away unsure of how he felt; sad the young boys had to die, glad that he had not had to kill them, guilty for not being stronger in defence of his island — in truth he was in turmoil. He wondered how he could continue in the Resistance as he would surely have to kill at some time in the near future.

**

A Young German Soldier

My twin brother and I have been locked in a farm shed. We took shelter here and were found by a man who was as surprised as we were when we came face to face. He could have killed us but he has locked the door. We never imagined this would happen to us. Our mother was against us joining the army but they welcomed us and all the other young men who enlisted. I have a bad feeling about this situation I don't know how we can survive. The Greek man who found us was visibly shocked when we crossed ourselves and begged for mercy on our knees. That was when his demeanour changed and he turned and left. We have tried to break out but it's too difficult. Maybe when he returns in the morning we can make a run for it. That's our only hope.

**

The Resistance became a stronger, more structured organisation, more secretive and stealthy as the Germans became more brutal and ruthless. Minas changed his attitude dramatically after a shocking German assault on a village where the villagers were accused of hiding men from the Resistance. The women were raped in front of their menfolk and the men were lined up and shot in front of their families before the village was torched. Coming across the remaining terrified and injured villagers Minas became so enraged he swore to God that he would hunt and kill the men responsible for this crime even if it meant his own death. With careful planning and observation of the troop that had carried out the attack, the Resistance was able to devise a plan to attack when they were sleeping and hopefully had fewer guards on patrol. It was long after midnight when the Cretan and Allied men surrounded the German camp. Two men were assigned to kill each of the guards, who had their throats cut swiftly and quietly. Many of the sleeping soldiers were sitting ducks and were easily slaughtered but soon their screams woke the other Germans and a bloody battle eventuated in which men from both sides were injured and killed.

The situation continued like this for much of the time the Germans were on Crete, neither side giving in to the other. Stories of bravery and valour were told all over the island. An elderly man was said to have killed a paratrooper with his walking stick as the luckless lad was suspended by his parachute ropes from an olive tree.

Members of the Resistance hid in the mountains and hunted for food and relied on each other and the villagers who would sometimes leave food for them in secret hiding places during the night. This was done at great risk to themselves but it demonstrated what courage and determination they had. Greek and Allied soldiers often became close friends and one such friendship developed between Minas and an Australian man named Alex McKinnon. They met after a rather nasty raid by the Cretans in which men from both sides were wounded and killed. Alex was badly injured by a gunshot wound to his upper thigh and fell to the ground, hitting his head on a rock and being rendered unconscious. He came to sometime later as he was being carried out of the line of fire by Minas. Minas had applied a tourniquet to his leg and carried him to a cave up in the mountains where other injured men were recovering. When the tourniquet was removed and the bleeding had stopped Minas gave him a drink of raki to help deaden the pain.

"There is a big risk of infection so I will have to remove the bullet," said Minas to Alex.

"Have you ever done that before?" Alex asked.

"Yes, yes, many times in the past few weeks," he replied.

"Okay, but can I have some more of that drink before you start, please?"

Minas gave Alex the bottle and said, "Take a big drink but don't drink it all; I need some for your wound."

Another man who had helped to bring the wounded men to safety passed Alex a piece of cloth to bite on and Minas began to extract the bullet. First he flushed the wound with raki and with the help of a pair of long-nosed pliers that had been soaking in raki he managed to remove the bullet without much trouble. Alex managed to bear the pain and keep still but when he saw Minas approaching with a large darning needle threaded with thick black cotton he fainted. He woke just as Minas applied the last of six rough stitches to keep the flesh together. Minas insisted that Alex drink some water and then he let him sleep.

Minas cared for Alex as if he was his brother, making sure he had plenty to drink when he was weak and drowsy and feeding him thick soup to keep him nourished when he was too sick to care. Although Alex was unwell his body was able to fight off the infection and he began to recover.

Early in the war women living in a nearby village provided food which was manna from heaven for these unfortunate men and helped to keep their spirits up. When they ate beans in red sauce or vegetables stuffed with rice and herbs it was like eating at home and they bragged about how well their wives and mothers could cook. These meals were few and far between but when they arrived the men shared the food and treated it as a delicacy. However as the war continued food became very scarce, rabbits were scant and small birds almost disappeared. Sometimes the men had to scavenge for insects and grubs, even eating grass and weeds. Once a large number of locusts swarmed on the island and the men roasted them and pretended they were eating prawns.

Once Alex's wound was almost healed and he was able to walk a little, Minas made him a crutch to assist his mobility. He was left with a very ugly scar but it was a small price to pay for his life. Alex felt that he owed his life to Minas for his dedicated care and swore that he would repay him in some way. They had become close friends, almost like brothers, during their time together up in the mountains.

One night as they sat together helping each other learn the other's language and laughing at each other as they tried to remember and pronounce words, Alex said, "When this war is over, if you would like to come to Australia I will help you to get there and settle because I owe you my life. If you had not helped me I would probably be dead. Efharisto poli." (Thankyou very much.)

"Thank you but I don't think I will ever leave Crete," said Minas.

"Well, we will keep in touch and if you change your mind you just let me know."

35

Minas and Irini, Melbourne 1950s

After the war ended Alex returned home where he began work for the new Australian car company which was making Australia's first car, the Holden. Alex bought one: it was the first car he owned and it cost him seven hundred and thirty-three pounds, which was a lot of money. He was very proud of his car and he drove every day to the Fishermans Bend factory where he was foreman on the assembly line. Alex was happy to be home and settled into his life again but he always had Minas on his mind.

His wife knew all about what had happened and she agreed that Alex may not have survived if Minas had not been so good to him. They were aware that many Europeans were suffering after the end of the war and wanted to do something to help them and show their appreciation. After making inquiries and much discussion, they agreed to get in touch with Minas and assist the family to migrate to Australia if they wanted. It was difficult for Alex to contact Minas but eventually a letter did reach him and after a lot of difficulty with language and mail problems, Alex and his wife offered to sponsor Minas and his family to migrate to Australia. Most of Europe was ravaged by the war and people were hungry and worried about the future. Minas decided that he would go to Australia but would probably return to Crete when things got better. His wife Irini was reluctant to leave Crete but for her two young sons she agreed.

In 1953 Minas Mavrikakis, his wife Irini and two little boys arrived by ship at Port Melbourne on a cold winter's day. Irini was horrified by the grey sky, the rain and the drab grey port and as they drove through the city, which was deserted on a Sunday, she said to her husband, "Where have you brought us? This is like the end of the world."

After living in a Greek village they were accustomed to seeing people out and about in the streets, especially on a Sunday, which was the day for Greek families to go out. In those days in Melbourne everything was closed on Sundays and people were usually at home after attending church in the morning.

Alex picked the little family up from the port in his Holden car and took them back to his house in Ascot Vale. The two men, who had not seen each other for several years, had tears in their eyes as they embraced. Alex had converted his garage into sleeping accommodation for the family and it was warm, comfortable and private. Alex's wife Mary was very welcoming to Minas and Irini and they became good friends even though there were language difficulties in the beginning. Irini was a good cook and was very willing to make this her responsibility while they lived with Alex, so most nights they ate Greek cuisine. The family loved the different food she cooked for them and wished she could stay forever. They shopped in the local strip shops nearby but there was a limit to the type of vegetables available.

"I will take you to a big market next week," said Mary, "maybe you can find what you want there." The following week Mary took Irini to the Victoria Market on the edge of the city of Melbourne. They travelled on the tram which ran along Mount Alexander Road through Parkville towards the city. As the tram rattled along they passed an enormous park which at the time housed a vast migrant settlement called Camp Pell. The camp consisted of Nissan huts providing temporary accommodation for newly arrived migrants from Europe. There were hundreds of people living there in the basic, unattractive corrugated iron huts which had very simple living conditions.

"What is that place?" asked Irini.

When Mary told her, Irini hugged her friend and thanked her again for helping herself and Minas and providing such a safe, comfortable home for them.

They arrived at the market which was the biggest Irini had ever seen. It stretched over two blocks and was mostly under cover. They shopped for fresh fruit and vegetables and Irini tried to buy olive oil for cooking. She was amazed to discover it was almost impossible to buy olive oil in Australia, except in a chemist shop.

"We don't use oil for cooking, we use butter or animal fat," said Mary.

Much of the produce Irini was used to in Crete was not available in Melbourne so they had to improvise with the basic vegetables at hand.

Mary was a frequent visitor to the market and asked several of the store holders she knew whether they had a vacancy for Minas, and one did. So it was at the Victoria Market that Minas first found work selling fruit and vegetables. After he received his first pay packet Alex met him after work and took him to the pub to celebrate and to meet his friends.

As they entered the bar Alex had his arm across Minas's shoulder. "This is the man who saved my life," he proudly told his friends.

The men slapped him on the back and gave him three cheers.

"We will all shout you a beer," said one of the men called Bluey.

"Why will they shout at me?" asked Minas in bewilderment.

"No they won't shout *at* you, they will shout you a beer — it means they will buy you a beer."

They all shouted him a beer then Minas found out that he was expected to shout them all a beer, which he did that once but never again.

"Sorry Alex, I don't like your beer and I don't think I will ever drink that much again, it made me very sick the next day. One day I will invite your friends to my home and I will give them a real drink, raki."

Alex laughed out loud and said, "What will they think when I tell them it was used to clean my wound and deaden the pain."

"I am sure they will like it anyway. Why is your friend with the red hair called Bluey?"

"Because he has red hair."

"Surely his name should be Reddy, why Bluey?"

"Don't know, that's just the way it is."

After a month of work Minas gave Irini money to buy new shoes for their two children, Christos and Stavros, and suggested she should buy something nice for herself. Irini was so pleased because it was such a long time since she had had any money for herself.

"Where can we buy the shoes?" Irini asked.

"I will take you to Puckle Street," said Mary. "We can walk there on

Saturday morning with the children. There is a good shoe shop where they will X-ray the children's feet to make sure that the shoes fit properly."

"I would like to buy myself a new hat, is there a hat shop?"

"Yes, there's a very good little millinery shop," replied Mary.

36

Shopping in Puckle Street

In the 1950s, Puckle Street at Moonee Ponds was a well-known shopping centre in the northern suburbs of Melbourne. The shops, which were two-storey buildings with a dwelling upstairs, were built in the latter half of the 1800s and provided the surrounding suburbs of Essendon and Ascot Vale with all that the housewives of the day could want on a day to day basis. The women dressed conservatively and most wore hat and gloves even to do the shopping. They could be seen carrying their baskets and string bags full of purchases, stopping to admire a new baby or have a friendly chat before hurrying home to prepare the evening meal of meat and three vegetables for their families.

The following Saturday morning Mary and Irini walked with the children to Puckle Street. As they neared their destination they needed to cross the railway track but the gates were closed as a train approached. It was a freight train from the country carrying many trucks of coal, grain, timber and cages of sheep. In the 1950s trains were used to transport produce from the country hence the huge number of trucks on the train. The children stood at the gate and tried to count the number of trucks but there were so many they soon lost count. When the train finally passed they had to wait for the signalman to climb down from his box and open the heavy railway gates by hand. The signalman was housed in an unusual building which was high off the ground. It had large windows in each of the four walls and a wooden staircase on the outside. He spent his day changing the signals and manually opening and closing the huge heavy gates across the railway line.

Puckle Street stretched about half a kilometre from the railway station at one end to Mount Alexander Road at the other end. Wide verandas with roofs embellished with iron lacework covered the footpaths so you could walk the whole length of the street and be protected from the weather.

The two women began to walk down the south side so that Mary could point out all the different shops. There was a double-fronted red brick post office flanked by two ornate staircases, two banks with large heavy doors and a big hardware store. The hardware shop sold an incredible number of things held in drawers on shelves reaching right up to the ceiling. A man climbed up a tall ladder on wheels to reach the drawers. They sold tiny tacks and enormous nails, wheelbarrows, china dinner sets, chamber pots, plants and wire netting. Whatever you wanted they had it and you could buy one nail or a whole box of nails if you wanted. Mary entered the shop and asked for six cup hooks and they all watched as the man pulled the ladder to the correct place and climbed halfway up to the shelf which had a drawer full of cup hooks. He wrapped them in brown paper and tied the parcel with string and said to Mary, "That will be one and six thank you" (one shilling and sixpence).

They passed a large stationery shop which also housed a lending library and further down the street there was an art deco picture theatre with posters advertising the weekly movie. The picture showing on that night was "Rear Window" starring Grace Kelly and James Stewart.

"Oh," said Irini, "Grace Kelly is so beautiful, she really does look like a princess."

They crossed over the road and began to walk back towards the railway line looking into every shop window as they went.

"The children will like this shop, it has something very unusual inside," said Mary as they entered a double-fronted shop called Love & Pollards, a very large store which sold clothes, manchester, haberdashery and many other bits and pieces.

Mary bought a pair of green and white striped towels and when Irini saw that there were blue and white striped towels as well, she bought a pair because they reminded her of the Greek flag.

"Now watch this," Mary said to the children.

The sales assistant took the money from Mary and wrote a receipt then she put both into a timber tumbler which she screwed into an apparatus hanging from the ceiling. She pulled a cord and the tumbler flew to the centre of the shop where a cashier sat in an elevated cage. The cashier removed the contents and put the change into the tumbler, screwed it into the apparatus, pulled a cord and it returned a few seconds later with the change and the handwritten receipt. Irini and her children were fascinated with this way of making a purchase and stood and watched while Irini's transaction went through.

"Okay, let's go," said Mary. "The shops shut at twelve, we must hurry if we are going to buy everything."

The next shop they entered was Kift's shoe shop where Irini bought lace-up shoes for her two boys. Before the sales assistant was satisfied with the fit she took the children behind a wall and X-rayed their feet. The children could see the bones in their feet so they wiggled their toes and watched in amazement. From the 1920s until the late 1950s it was common practice to use this method to fit children's shoes. Children stood with their feet in a box called a fluoroscope and the X-ray clearly showed the bones of the feet.

They entered a butcher shop which had a thick layer of sawdust covering the floor. The butcher gave each of the children a slice of sausage which he handed to them on the point of a huge sharp knife. Next door there was a fish shop where Irini bought some fish she had never seen before called flathead. The children stood outside and watched the fresh water cascading down the inside of the window to keep the fish cold. Further along there was a furniture store called Nunan's which sold the latest furniture of the 1950s. Mary looked in and secretly wished that she would be able to buy the furniture in the window one day.

"Now Irini," said Mary, grabbing her hand, "something for you. The hat shop I mentioned."

It was a small-fronted shop with shiny brass trim around the windows; in the smaller window there was just one hat sitting on a wooden hat stand and in the slightly larger window on the other side of the door two hats were displayed.

"Are you sure they will have a hat for me? They don't seem to have many," said Irini.

"Yes, they will have a hat to suit you I'm sure. Let's go in."

There were two doors and as they went through the first door a bell rang before the other door was reached and they entered a very quiet, softly lit shop. There were several lamps lighting the shop and it gave the impression of elegance and quality. The shop sold hats, gloves and scarves for women.

A quiet woman welcomed them and asked the children to sit on the floor near the door telling them that they would be given a lolly if they sat quietly.

"Do I have enough money for this shop?" whispered Irini.

"Yes, you have plenty. Minas gave you five pounds — that is quite a large amount."

Irini chose a beautiful dark blue felt hat decorated with blue cross-grain ribbon and small red berries. She loved it so much she kept it on. The hat was paid for and the children received their lollies as they left the shop and the bell rang behind them.

"I have money left over," said Irini. "I would like to buy paints and brushes for Minas to start painting again. Is there a shop that sells such things?"

There was a large Coles store which sold all sorts of items so they went there and bought the paint and brushes and headed for home very happy with the morning's shopping.

As they neared the railway station a train from the city had just pulled out. A small crowd of well-dressed men and women walked down the ramp towards several gleaming black carriages pulled by beautifully groomed black horses. Irini noticed that most of the passengers carried binoculars and looked very important as they boarded the carriages which set off clip-clopping down Puckle Street.

"Where are they going?" Irini asked.

"There is a racecourse called Moonee Valley over the main road where a Saturday race meeting is held once a month. They will be hoping to win some money on the horses. Good luck I say."

When they returned home Minas was pleased to see Irini's hat and was happy to see his children in good strong shoes again. Tears filled his eyes when Irini presented him with the paint and brushes and that afternoon he began to paint again.

Because Minas was an artist Alex told him about the National Gallery in the city and promised to take him. He also told him about the Archibald Prize for portraits held every year in Australia and suggested he should enter a painting. Minas was instantly attracted to the idea but said that he had one picture in his head from his time in the Resistance which he had to paint first and then he would think about painting a portrait of Alex to enter in the competition.

The next weekend the two families went into the city on the tram to visit the National Gallery of Victoria. It was situated in a beautiful building in Swanston Street and also housed the State Library and the Melbourne Museum. While Alex and Minas viewed the paintings the children went with their mothers to the museum area. There were dioramas of all types of animals and birds in their natural habitats, bones of dinosaurs, stuffed tigers, insects and wonderful miniature machines in glass display cases where you could push a button and see the machinery work.

The men viewed the Australian art and Minas was very taken with a huge painting by Frederick McCubbin called The Pioneers. The painting was a triptych: one canvas divided into three panels. A young man with his new bride was depicted in the first section, several years later the two of them now with a child in the second section and the third picture showed the grown child looking at a grave. Minas was very moved by the painting and sat and looked at it for quite a while. He thought it a wonderful way to tell a story and decided this was how he would paint the picture from his time in the Resistance which he could not erase from his memory.

"This painting has given me an idea for the one I have in my head," he told Alex. "Now I know how I will paint it."

The following week Minas prepared a large canvas and began by dividing it into three sections. He was not able to work on the painting for long periods because the subject caused him some anxiety. Sometimes he would cover it and leave it for weeks at a time then work at it for twelve hours nonstop. Because of a decision he had never had to make, the third panel was proving difficult for him to complete.

37

Peaceful life, 1960s-1970s

Minas and Irini's children Christos and Stavros went to the local state primary school with Alex and Mary's two girls Carole and Beth. The girls were fiercely protective of the two boys as they struggled to learn the language, cope with the school work and fit in with the different cultural attitudes. A close friendship had developed between all the members of the two families so there was some sadness felt when Minas announced that it was time for them to move into their own home. He had saved a lot of money and was able to put a deposit on a small timber house in Moonee Ponds. The house was a bit old and run down and in need of an update but it was their own home and they loved it.

Once they had settled into their new house Minas contacted his family in Crete and asked for some of his paintings to be shipped to Australia. Once the paintings arrived and he was able to see that it could be done, he began negotiating to import olive oil into Australia. It took a long time to organise but it eventually happened and people could buy large tins of olive oil for cooking in Australia. Minas sold the oil at the market and built up a good strong business selling not only to Greeks but to other European migrants as well.

The children finished primary school and went to the local secondary school for the next six years of their education. Christos then went to teachers' college and Stavros went to work as a teller in the State Savings Bank of Victoria. Carole trained as a kindergarten teacher and Beth began to train as a nurse at the Royal Melbourne Hospital.

The two families remained good friends and the parents saw each other often but the children rarely saw each other as they all went their separate ways. One Easter Minas and Irini decided to celebrate in the traditional Greek way with a lamb on a spit on Easter Sunday. Carole brought her fiancé and Stavros brought his girlfriend. Christos and Beth, who were both single, came alone. They had not seen each other for several years and were pleased to rekindle the friendship. They spent most of the day together and found they were attracted to each other and Christos asked her to go out with him the following weekend. They began going out together and were engaged to be married by the end of the year. Their parents were so happy to think that the two families would now be related by marriage and between them they organised a wonderful wedding. First they had to establish where the couple would marry: that is, which church — the Greek Orthodox Church or the Methodist Church. Beth wanted to be married in a garden to prevent any arguments, Christos and his parents wanted the service to be in the Greek Orthodox Church and Alex and Mary wanted the Methodist Church. After a lot of discussion, some of it quite passionate, it was decided that because Beth's family owed Minas so much for saving Alex's life they would agree to his wishes. However there was a condition; that a Methodist Minister would also marry them. The Greek priest insisted that he performed his service first because then they would be married in God's eyes in the Greek way.

Most of the Australian guests had never been inside a Greek church and found it very interesting, specially the crowns which were passed backwards and forwards between the heads of the bride and groom, and the way bride and groom walked around the altar three times. The wedding reception was a simple but tasteful dinner dance where some of the Greek guests pinned money onto Beth's dress as she danced. Both Alex and Minas made brief speeches mentioning their love and respect for each other.

The couple drove to the Gold Coast for their honeymoon and enjoyed two weeks of beach in the morning, lovemaking in the afternoon and wining and dining each night. On their return to Melbourne the newlyweds rented a flat in Essendon and life resumed its normal routine.

Beth continued to work as a nurse and Christos taught in the secondary school where they had all been students.

Minas built up his business and now imported olives and cheese and some other tinned foods which were not available in Australia. He began to devote weekends to painting and finally completed a portrait of Alex even though he had not yet completed the third panel of his triptych. The portrait was so good that Alex persuaded Minas to enter it in the Archibald portrait competition, which he did; it did not win but was highly commended. The three-panelled painting on which Minas continued to work was a constant thorn in his side because he just could not complete the third panel.

Christos and Beth bought a small Victorian terrace house in Essendon and began to restore and renovate, as was the new trend in Melbourne. They enjoyed painting and decorating the interior and fixing the overgrown garden in an attempt to get the 'cottage garden' style which suited the house.

Beth returned from work one night and said, "I am going to start on the second bedroom because we will need it for a nursery early in November."

"A baby — are we having a baby? Why didn't you tell me earlier?"

"I just wanted to be sure so I had a pregnancy test at the staff clinic this week and it took a couple of days to get the result. Would you believe they inject the urine into a female frog and if it produces eggs within twenty-four hours that's a positive result?"

Christos grabbed Beth and hugged her. "I'm sorry for the frog but I am so happy we are having a baby!"

"Yes I am so excited, I can hardly wait," Beth laughed.

"If it's a boy he will be named Minas of course," said Christos.

"I don't know about that, do we have to continue with that tradition?"

"I would really like to name my son after my father."

"Well he could be Minas Alexander after both our fathers, but what if it's a girl?"

"You can call her any name you choose as long as we name our son Minas.

"A girl will be Poppy. I love floral names for girls and Poppy is my favourite."

Beth's pregnancy was healthy and was followed by the quick, uneventful delivery of a beautiful baby boy. The baby had a hearty appetite and sucked hungrily at his mother's breast as often as he needed then fell into long exhausted sleep. He was a perfect baby and Beth was besotted with him.

Beth's mother Mary asked why he was not circumcised. "Isn't it cleaner?"

"No Mum, it's not cleaner and it's not necessary, and it's not done to Greek babies."

"Well when you were born I know all the baby boys were done on the third day."

"That was in the 1940s: now we are in the 1970s we know better and it's not done unless there is a medical or religious reason."

"Well, I hope you know what you are doing."

Baby Minas was a delightful child who laughed and played and made his parents very happy. Minas senior was thrilled to have his grandson named after him. He had wondered, now that they lived in Australia and his son had married an Australian woman, whether the custom would continue.

38

Poppy is born, 1980

A second child, Poppy, was born two years after baby Minas. She was a bundle of giggles and curls and by two years of age she was the boss of her older brother and had her parents totally smitten. The grandparents were all keen to babysit as often as they were asked and Beth was able to resume work part time as a nurse when Poppy was two years old.

When Poppy was quite young her love of animals became apparent and she always had several pets, most of them rescued from somewhere. Chickens that were hatched at kinder, kittens no one wanted to adopt from school friends, dogs that were too active for their elderly owners and the white mice from the science room at school. When she was about 15 years old her father woke her early one morning,

"Poppy, there is a visitor to see you outside."

"I don't want to get up yet, I want to sleep in, who is it?"

"You had better come and see, I think you will be pleasantly surprised."

Poppy pulled on her dressing gown and went outside and there was a very fat bandy-legged goose standing in the driveway. The poor thing had been abandoned in a nearby park and was terrified of the wide open spaces. Why it had come to Poppy's place no one knew, but it had definitely come to the right place. They made inquiries and discovered it had been the pet of a family who had kept it in a small cage for which it had grown too big. They did not want it any more so just left it in the park near a lake. Poppy and her mother tried to release it several times but the terrified goose waddled over to them and sheltered behind Poppy's legs. They took it to another park with a bigger lake and a flock of geese but it was not interested in either of these things and once again hid behind Poppy's legs.

"It's terrified," said Poppy. "We will just have to take it home and keep the poor thing."

The goose was a female who they called Lucy and she laid a dozen huge white eggs in early spring in appreciation for being in such a kind home. Whenever Poppy sat outside under the apple tree reading, Lucy would lay her head on her lap and look up at her in adoration. Poppy stroked her head and called her Lucy The Goosey. Thinking Lucy would benefit from some goose company Poppy went to the market and bought two goslings. The yellow goslings were very pleased to meet Lucy but she didn't know what they were and ran away from them. The more she ran the more they chased her, wanting the protection of a parent figure. It took several days before Lucy realised they were okay and she finally settled down and enjoyed their company.

When Poppy finished secondary school she went to Melbourne University to study Veterinary Science and during orientation week she met Mike. He was a tall, good-looking man with fair hair, blue eyes and a big friendly smile. They hit it off immediately and were together for the whole time at university. The relationship, which began like so many others, started in love and lust and became one of mostly friendship, love and a nice habit. Mike had an uncle who owned a veterinary practice in Greenmount, a semi-rural township outside Melbourne. The uncle was only too keen to have both Mike and Poppy work with him during the latter years of their studies. After they qualified and had been working for two years he offered the practice to them at a reasonable price. It was an offer too good to refuse and both sets of parents helped the young couple to buy the business. Poppy worked hard until her trip to Greece with her friend Sophia where she met George and he changed her life.

39

Solving the problem

Poppy's father talked for hours relating the story of his family to the young couple. Poppy and George listened without asking any questions; they were both fascinated with the story and with the idea that they were most likely related to the family who had survived over one hundred years ago way back in Kasos.

"What a wonderful story," said Poppy. "Thanks Dad for putting it all together for us."

"Well it's for all of us and for George's parents also."

"I will ring my parents tonight and tell them, I'm sure they will be thrilled," said George. "They have the other part of the story and now we can make it one big saga which I will write so everyone can read it."

"You can't write it yet because we have to finish the story by deciding where we are going to live, here or in Greece," said Poppy.

Christos interrupted, "I have spoken to a friend who teaches in one of the Greek schools in Melbourne, he says he may be able to assist you with an interview for a teaching position."

"Okay, I will go to the school and see if they offer me a position but I cannot promise anything until that happens," replied George.

"I want to you to look at the painting again before you go," Christos took George into the study. "I want you to see now what caused my father so much anxiety while he painted it."

Hanging on the wall was the three-panelled canvas Minas had painted, depicting two identical teenage boys creeping into an outhouse, the boys on their knees begging for mercy and in the third panel the two boys up in a flower-filled mountain meadow tending a herd of goats.

40

Resolution

George attended the Greek school for an interview and was subsequently offered a position too good to refuse, so the decision was made much easier for him. Naturally Poppy was thrilled and so were all her family members. It was decided they would marry in Kasos next year in the Greek summer. George went home to resign from his job and prepare his parents for his decision to stay in Australia.

The following year in June the whole family travelled to Kasos for the wedding; they went early so they could take part in the remembrance celebration for the 1824 massacre on June 7 in Kasos. There were many visitors from Athens, America, Canada and Australia who arrived to take part in the annual celebration. George's parents provided a place for the wedding guests to stay as there was not enough hotel accommodation available. This turned out to be a good thing because they all spent a lot of time together talking and were able to piece together their two family stories.

George's mother realised she had to accept the marriage between George and Poppy and their decision to live in Australia because it was going to happen no matter what she thought. Once she made friends with Poppy's family she mellowed and embraced them and the wedding plans. The couple promised to return to Kasos each summer to visit family and to help at the taverna.

Poppy's brother Minas who had been living in Berlin arrived with his German girlfriend a few days before the wedding. He had not seen his family for more than a year and they had not met his girlfriend, Eva. They announced their intention to marry also but they would be marrying in Australia and living in Germany.

"Oh well, you can't have it all your own way," said George's mother, smiling mischievously.

Poppy's two grandfathers from Australia and George's grandfather from Kasos spent many hours sitting together talking about what had happened in Kasos and in Crete, Egypt and Australia; about their children and grandchildren, the government, fishing and just about anything else they could think of until they fell asleep in the warm sun. When they woke they would start all over again. One day the two young couples observed the three grandfathers discussing the Second World War in Crete. It began when one of them brought along a bottle of raki, which they were halfway through. Alex dropped a glass and as he picked up the pieces he cut his finger quite badly. He held his hand out for the other two to see and Minas poured his raki over the wound.

"Ouch," yelled Alex, "Not that again."

Then the story of Minas rescuing Alex began amid laughter and a loud discussion about the healing properties of raki and ended with Alex showing the scar on his leg to the small gathering. The men commented on the size of the zig-zag scar which was high on Alex's thigh. It still showed signs of an untrained hand at work. "He stitched it up with a darning needle," joked Alex.

"I have never seen the scar before; he always kept it hidden," said Poppy. "He must be feeling very relaxed."

The warm sun and the raki soon quietened the three old men and they dozed off.

Eva asked about the scar on Alex's leg and when she heard them mention Crete during the Second World War, she listened with interest and then became very quiet.

"What is it Eva?" said Poppy. "Have we said something to upset you?"

"Well, my grandfather was also in Crete during the war with his two young brothers who were killed on the island very soon after they arrived. The family always said what a mistake it was to allow three brothers to be involved in a war in the same place at the same time. The two younger ones were identical twins and their mother never recovered from their deaths."

41

A wedding on Kasos, 2012

The days were hot but there was always a gentle breeze blowing in from the sea. The Mavrikakis families were usually up early for breakfast together before the sun got too hot. They sat out on the terrace and ate fresh pastries, fruit and lots of coffee before a walk to the beach for those who were not working, followed by a siesta in the afternoon. Each night was a noisy, fun-filled time of dancing, singing and lots of laughter before a late-night stroll back to their accommodation.

The nights were warm and the air was filled with the sound of chirping insects and fluttering moths that made easy pickings for the hungry owls that swept rapidly to and fro.

At 5pm on the Sunday following the remembrance celebration, George and Poppy were married in the little church in Free. The day was hot but as usual a cool breeze blew in from the nearby sea. Inside the church it was quiet and cool. People whispered as they entered, lit a candle, crossed themselves and sat to wait for the bride to arrive.

Poppy looked radiant, the epitome of a happy bride, wearing a simple flowing white dress that reached just below her knees. The narrow shoulder straps were covered by a lace wrap to cover her décolletage whilst in the church. A wreath of white flowers interwoven with wildflowers adorned her hair.

As Poppy walked to the church on her father's arm the women sang a wedding song about a girl who is getting married today.

Semera ga, Simera gamos ginette. Semera ga, simera gamos ginette.
Se oreo perivoli, Se oreo perovoli.
Today a wedding is taking place,
In a beautiful garden
Today a mother will be separated from her daughter.
The groom will love his wife and not admonish her,
The groom will admire his wife as he would admire the precious
basil flower.
Up, up, fly like an eagle, open your wings and fly.
Hold your precious dove in your embrace.

The church was shaded by a large tree whose canopy reached from one side of the churchyard to the other, sheltering the little whitewashed courtyard and making it a cool refuge from the sun. Colourful saints decorating the interior of the church stared from sightless eyes at the congregation and newly lit candles burned brightly near the altar. The church was close enough to the sea to hear gulls and the occasional call of fishermen during the wedding service.

George's face lit up in a smile of love and pride when he saw Poppy enter the church on her father's arm and he did not take his eyes off her until she stood beside him at the front of the church. Poppy looked at George and smiled.

The kindly priest performed the ceremony in Greek interspersed with a little English where he was able. As they walked out into the bright sunshine arm in arm, bells rang and people threw flowers on to the delighted couple as they walked along the road to the Taverna Feggari. Young girls and children laughed and ran ahead as everyone sang the wedding song again. The evening was perfect for an outdoor wedding celebration which went well into the early hours of the morning.

George's father presented the couple with an old book which was covered in worn fabric and had the words 'BIBLIO-PAPA' embroidered on the cloth cover.

"This is in your care now and for you to pass on to your son or daughter in the future. This is a real family heirloom," he said. "We think you deserve to own the book because now that you have married you have reunited the family which was torn apart by the results of the massacre on our beautiful island."

Poppy and George were aware of the book and the significance of it to the family and felt privileged to accept it. "We will treasure the Biblio-Papa," said Poppy.

When Poppy and George were finally able to leave they were serenaded up the road to the little windmill house where they fell into bed exhausted. As sleep swept over them they were soothed by the constant sound of gentle waves lapping at the shore of the island of Kasos.